WIDOW'S ISLAND

M. LEE PRESCOTT

For my family, always, with love.

CHAPTER 1

"You can't send that nitwit Peterson to do the job. Jesus, Marty! The last census we sent him out on was so fucked up it had to be completely redone."

"Then who do you suggest, Phil? Margot's on Block Island 'till August and Ray's wife'd never cut him loose for that long; six months is a long time to be away from the family. That's why Andy'd be so perfect. No wife, no kids, practically no friends, and…"

"Forget it. I'll call Ned. He's the best person for the job anyway."

"Fielding—you gotta be kidding! Penny'd never let him out of his cage for six months!"

"Penny's got nothin' to do with it—they're separated."

"Too bad…I didn't know. Not that it's a surprise; mismatched couple of the century, if you ask me. Mrs. Society and Mr. Limpet. Geez, how'd they ever hook up in the first place?"

"Married when they were kids; baby already on the way. Some people grow up together in those kinda marriages. Some don't. Anyway, Ned'd be glad of the chance to get away, I'll bet. It's been pretty nasty on the home front from what he tells me."

"Still under the same roof? Thought you said separated?"

"He's lookin', but they're still sharing the house. She's away right now, I think, with orders for him to be gone before she gets back. His family's house, you know.

'Bout the only thing he brought to the marriage and Penny wants it. Sickening when you think of all the Pardington millions she has to throw around."

"Good old Ned. Penny's always been a bitch."

"Marty, I haven't got time for this right now," the older man interrupted, feeling like a traitor for gossiping about his friend's marriage. "I'll call Ned and if he can't go, better start packing. Someone's gotta be on the Winward Island by the middle of the month. Nicrophorus americanus, if they're there, will be emerging by then and we want a complete study covering the whole six months till dormancy."

"I'll be in Portsmouth if you need me. Later, Phil."

Marty Robinson left his friend to sort through the disheveled mess on his desk. Phil couldn't remember Ned Fielding's phone number, didn't keep a rolodex or an address book, and his blotter, where the number was jotted down, was buried under a mountain of papers. Shifting the pile back and forth several times, he peeked cautiously underneath each corner. As he moved towards the middle of the blotter, he started a landslide of bills, flyers and grant proposals. The pile picked up steam, scooping up an overburdened vertical file in a downward rush. "Shit!" he muttered, watching the last of the papers cascade over the floor, some coming to rest under the water cooler, others floating into an open aquarium. "Sorry Boris," he said, lunging to remove a stack of Chace Point Bird Sanctuary brochures from the back of a baby snapping turtle, too startled by the sudden onslaught to snap at him.

Turning back to the desk, he spied Fielding's number scribbled on the now-emptied blotter. He dialed. Busy. Leaning back, he closed his eyes for several minutes. It had been a hard year for SENCA, the Southeastern Natural Conservation Agency, of which he was president. The whole region was in a recession and state and federal funding had been slashed. The first thing to go had been Phil's secretary, Edna, who had been with him since the beginning—almost twenty years. They'd been good years, he reflected. He missed Edna. Actually, she'd been ready to retire and he just hadn't bothered to replace her. He could easily hire part-time help, but he figured he'd save money and besides, he hated to break in a new person and have her poking around in his and Edna's stuff.

And SENCA was in better shape than most. They had a generous endowment—lots of folks remembered them in their wills and the money had been invested prudently. King Barlow's gift alone would keep them in operation for twenty or thirty years. And, in addition to the money, he had bequeathed Winward Island—half of it anyway—to the agency in his will. The island had been the one holding they'd neglected, until now.

On an unauthorized day trip, a couple of college kids, SENCA volunteers, had discovered what they believed to be Giant Carrion beetles, nicrophorus americanus, on the island. A rare species of burying beetles, nicrophorus americanus had thought to be extinct until their discovery in recent years on Block Island. Now they might also be present on Winward—the importance of this study dictated that he must send a decent researcher. Ned Fielding was overqualified for this type of field study, but the only man within the agency whom Phil trusted to do the job right.

They hadn't sent anyone to the island since its acquisition twelve years earlier. It was time to conduct a complete census of the plant and animal life, time to map it out and give the island the attention it deserved. Its location along the Atlantic Flyway alone made it an important, extremely valuable acquisition.

He tried Fielding again. This time the phone rang four times before Ned picked it up.

"Ned, hey, it's Phil."

"Hi Phil!"

"How are things going?"

"'Bout the same. You know about Penny and me, there's not much more to say."

"It's been great having your help at Chace Point this spring. Wish we could pay you more, but…"

"Hey, I've enjoyed myself. Ray and I just got the nest platform up on the spit—East Marsh—and we're lookin' for a new project."

"That's the reason I'm calling. You got a place to live yet, buddy?"

"I think I've got a place out near Watuppa Pond—friend of a friend. Gonna rent for a while, 'till I get things straightened out. Why?"

"Well, if you're free to get away for awhile, I have a job for you. Winward Island. Ever heard of it?"

"Yeah, off the coast near Derryville. Barrier Island—we own it, don't we? SENCA, I mean."

"Yup—it's one of our few undiscovered frontiers. We need a complete census, soil samples, beach study, and surveying. Giant Carrion beetles have been found out there, you know."

"No, I didn't. Wow! After Block Island, that should be…"

"Let me qualify my statement. Grad students may have found the beetles last summer. They took some pretty amazing photos, no samples though, just pictures. Only there a few hours. Typical. But listen, buddy, if they're there, we could work with the Block Island people on a recovery plan to bring them back. We need you for that, Ned. What do you say—you game?"

"Sounds good. How much time you talking about?"

"At least six months, maybe more."

"Phil, I'd love to, but…with the divorce and all, I'm not sure I could get away for that long. Can I get back to you later?"

"Sure. I can give you a couple of days, but don't wait too long, buddy. Someone's gotta be out there by the middle of the month, and I'll have to get Peterson or Ray if you can't."

"I'll let you know tomorrow. Thanks Phil."

CHAPTER 2

Ned debated an hour or two before calling Penny at the beach house to which she had retreated—until he "vacated her home." She reacted with typical venom, but Ned, stoic and unmoved, ignored her. They had been living apart emotionally for so many years, a few extra months wouldn't hurt before their ties were legally severed. He just didn't care anymore. Didn't care if she took the house, the antiques, the dog—although he'd miss Haggardy. Penny didn't even like Haggardy. She was keeping him for spite.

"I can't believe how selfish you are, Ned. But then you've always put yourself first, before me, before the kids, before your social obligations, before everything. For God sakes, couldn't you think of me for just this once? How am I going to get on with my life if you leave me dangling here for six months while you're off counting bugs?!"

"Do you want to get remarried right away, Penny?"

"Are you kidding? After what you put me through, I'll never marry again!"

"Then what does it matter, really? Six months isn't long after all the years we've…"

"Don't even say it Ned! I will not have our estrangement become public knowledge. In fact, I'm having Martin draw up gag orders to that effect. I will not have my reputation ruined by gossip and I'll thank you to speak to no one about our affairs, past or present, until the papers are drawn up."

"Penny, relax. Everyone knows. It's not exactly a surprise. Can we just let it go for now? I'm going to Winward and I'll be back the end of October, beginning of November. We can sign papers then, or if you can't wait, I can come back for a day to take care of things whenever you and Martin have things ready."

"What about the settlement?" What about all the details, the division of property, the…"

"You handle it Pen. Whatever you think is fair. Have it all if you want. I…"

"Isn't that typical! Once again, I have to do it all. Isn't there anything you want?"

"My clothes, tools, and…"

"Yes…here it comes. I knew it."

"Well, if you'd like, I could take Haggardy. He's a…"

"Forget it! Just forget it, Ned! I wouldn't dream of sending Haggardy to some God forsaken island, probably loaded with deer ticks and fleas! Besides, he belongs to me."

"Fine, Pen. Listen—I gotta go. I'll send you an address where I can be reached and I'll call the kids too."

"That's the other thing, the children. Are they supposed to wait six months too; to have this settled, to see you, to…?"

"I'll call them, Penny. If they have strong objections, I won't go, okay? Now, I've really got to go."

"Fine, I'm late for an appointment! You'll be hearing from Martin soon. Good-bye."

She clicked the phone down before he could say good-bye, anything to get the last word.

He put off calling the kids until the evening, but he called Phil and accepted the job. Neither Ned Jr. nor Sydney, his daughter, would care, he knew, but he'd check with them anyway.

CHAPTER 3

Icy pearls of sunlit water fell noiselessly from the paddles as the kayak glided through the channel rounding the east end of Winward Island. With spring, Addie spent her mornings, just after sunrise, paddling in the marshes. A net and several empty burlap bags lay ready, stuffed in the prow beside her feet, should they be needed. But pleasure, not work, drove her to the sea in the early morning hours.

The day was clear and crisp. The April morning air embraced her with cloying chilliness. The marsh beckoned, reaching out to envelop her in its magical green depths, but thoughts intruded, distracting her from the rustling beauty that surrounded her. Usually, she paddled hard for a time, then lifted the paddles and drifted, listening to the sea birds screeching and calling, the fish jumping and the rustle of the spartina…soft and soothing, but today she paddled ferociously as if driven by unseen demons, faster and faster until beads of sweat dotted her brow and her arms burned with the strain of exertion.

Her home was about to be invaded and there was absolutely nothing she could do about it. For twelve years, she had lived alone on the island. Now her sanctuary, her peaceful world was to be taken over, perhaps forever. Who would they send? Would there be more than one? Would they disregard the boundaries and trespass onto her side of the island?

The trustees of her husband's estate had assured her that the conservation agency that shared the island with her would respect her privacy. They owned thirty acres, she twenty. The island was to be kept as a wildlife sanctuary. No building, no camping, no human habitation was planned for Winward Island, the name they had given it upon taking possession. Now they were sending someone to live for six months on her island. Six months!

She knew she was lucky to have the land at all. So many times over those last precarious months, King had threatened to take it away, threatened to will the entire island to SENCA and let them have her cottage, her gardens, everything. He'd laughed and taunted her continuously, knowing that Winward was her only refuge, her only love. She didn't love him, had never loved him. But, King Barlow had died suddenly before he could change his will and his widow had inherited the cottage and its surrounding acreage, the fields, ponds, gardens and thicket. She owned the cove with its many caves hidden beneath the cliffs, where she loved to explore.

The dock was in the cove, the only easy access to the island, hence the reason SENCA had contacted her in the first place, to request permission to use her dock. Recognizing the futility of refusing, she had written back giving her consent and requested that they use the west footpath to reach their property, rather than the more direct path running north to south that traversed her fields. The reply assured her that the agency would respect her privacy, keeping to the western footpath when venturing forth from the dock. "Rest easy Mrs. Barlow," the letter had ended. "Our people will try not to pester you in the slightest way. We are as eager as you are to ensure that Winward remains undisturbed and peaceful. Please contact me personally if there is any problem whatsoever. Phillip K Bodington, director SENCA."

The letter from Mr. Bodington had not reassured her, especially the part about "our people." Was there to be a whole bevy of scientists crawling over the island for six months? Would there also be a steady stream of visitors taking part in the study? Visions of boatloads of college students descending upon Winward made her shudder and the paddle jabbed unevenly beneath the glassy surface of the water, the handle nearly jerking free of her grasp.

Glimpsing a crab, its broad swimming legs catching the sunlight as he paddled sideways through the eel grass, she swung the net, a flawless extension of her right arm and scooped him up, wetting the burlap bag with her left hand as she tossed him in. The action, completed in a few seconds time, appeared to be almost reflexive, after which she continued paddling, worries consuming her still.

After an hour's time, she headed back, a bag full of crabs, heart and mind no lighter, but resigned. Dropping the crabs in one of the pots near shore, she paddled in and pulled the kayak up onto the beach. She kept her fishing scow tied to the dock, but she preferred to drag the lighter craft up onto the beach. That way it could be more easily be carried to higher ground if a storm threatened or she could drag it over the ridge for use in the pond near the cottage. She scanned the surface of the water closely for some minutes before turning to head up the path lined with rose hips and honeysuckle that led back to the cottage.

As she entered the thicket, she heard a familiar screech. She turned in time to spy a huge bird dropping from the vast blue above her, its talons outstretched as it fell. Pulling a leather glove from her pocket, she slipped it onto her right hand, stretching her arm out straight to her side. Sharp talons dug into the leather as the osprey came to rest, grasping her gloved hand. "Gwydyon, son of Don," she smiled, stroking his feathers, "How goes it with you this fine day?"

The fish hawk bowed his head, enjoying the attention, alternately gazing from his mistress to the sea. "I have nothing for you this morning, maybe later." As she talked, she walked slowly along the path through the thicket. When it became clear that no meal was forthcoming, Gwydyon became restless. "Just a minute my friend," she cooed, quickening her pace.

Vulnerable to attack in the thicket, she hated to release him lest his flight be checked by an unforeseen enemy. Without food, he was probably safe, but there were several golden eagles and great horned owls that frequented the island. While they rarely challenged Gwydyon on the open water where he was pestered instead by terns continually lying in wait to steal his catch—they might hazard a skirmish in the brush where his sharp, lashing talons were less effective.

Finally, she reached the open fields. From there, the path ran straight through the meadows to the shingled cottage just visible in the distance. The bird arched his wings, rearing back. Addie released him with an upward thrust and his powerful wings carried him aloft. As soon as he reached a safe height, he circled once, screeching farewell as he disappeared over the treetops towards the open sea.

Walking on, she stared ahead at the whitewashed cottage, her home for the past twelve years. Built seventeen years earlier, at the time of her marriage, the cottage had been winterized when Addie had settled permanently on the island. Two stories with a wide porch wrapped permanently around its front and sides, the faded white shingled walls were alive with climbing greenery, English ivy crept high under the second story windows intertwined with clematis vines, the blue and white flowers not yet in bloom. The vegetation at first gave the impression of wild abandon, belying the hours of cultivation and care that had put them there.

A two-story barn with a lean-to shed and greenhouse attached stood behind the house to the south. The land gently sloped from the back of the cottage so that the taller, more imposing barn faded gracefully into the receding landscape, rather than overwhelming the much smaller house. Its brown, weathered sides blended comfortably with the woods to the east, at harmony with its surroundings.

As she approached the cottage, a yelp of greeting hailed her as a tawny beast bounded up flinging her front paws around her mistress. Laughing, Addie knelt beside her pet, ruffling the soft fur on the animal's back. "Aran! So you finally decided to wake up! No swim for you this morning!"

Woman and beast went together into the cottage where she fed her pet, fixing tea for herself. Sipping it slowly, she sat at the worn table fashioned with her own hands from wood carted back from the mainland by boat. There was a salvage yard in Derryville she visited when she needed materials for the house and she kept an old pick-up truck on the mainland to use for these infrequent sojourns and for her deliveries of produce and fish. She hated driving, but as her client list had grown, the truck had become indispensable. The drop-off places along the river reached roughly half of her customers; the rest had to be delivered by truck.

During the spring, her days were freer; the garden was not yet in full flower and the fishing still sparse. The Massachusetts climate demanded caution in planting fragile, warm weather crops, but her tomatoes, peppers, eggplants and flowers were flourishing in the warm moisture of the greenhouse. She attended to them first, passing among the rows to give water and pinch back unwanted growth. The greenhouse, too, had been built entirely from salvage materials. Unlike the cottage and barn that her former husband had had built—as a wedding gift to her—the greenhouse and shed had been constructed later on, after she had come to live on the island.

The first years she had survived on the small inheritance King had left her, tending a tiny garden for her own needs. When she began fishing, clamming, and lobstering to earn money, she expanded the garden too. Once she began marketing her produce, she needed a hothouse. Rather than hiring someone to build it, she had undertaken the project herself. It had saved money, but more importantly, it had given her confidence and a feeling of self-sufficiency. Previously she had called upon plumbers, carpenters, electricians and mechanics when things broke and needed repair, but since the completion of the shed and greenhouse ten years earlier, not another soul had set foot on the island. Whatever expertise she required came from books and her own experimentation.

Mid-day found her weeding and picking early spinach. She had already harvested parsnips and winter carrots and her broccoli, cauliflower and lettuces were well underway. She protected the lettuces at night and when the days were particularly cold, but the thick layer of mulch and the protected enclosure of the garden kept the plants relatively safe from a killing frost.

Until June she sold little of her produce, as most of her clients were seasonal residents, coming to spend the summer at the beach. She had a few year round customers that paid to have anything from her garden yield, as well as a share of her catch. What little money she made before June, however, came from the fish she sold to wholesalers. From June to October she sold only to her regular customers, unless there was a surplus. When summer cottages on the mainland coast were boarded up, she slowed down, moving into her winter schedule.

As the years went by, her customer list grew until she finally had to turn people away. She kept a waiting list of would-be customers only too eager to receive some of her weekly bounty; some offering double or triple the usual charge to be put "on the route." Addie refused to grow bigger, however, since the thought of having to hire help was abhorrent to her.

Each customer received three deliveries a week of fish, vegetables, herbs, flowers and fruit. They paid a flat, weekly fee, the same no matter what they received. When a new customer was taken on, they filled out a form with likes and dislikes. At that time, they selected which plan they desired; only fruit and vegetables, all five items—fish, vegetables, fruit, herbs and flowers, or just fish and flowers. While she attempted to cater to individual tastes, Addie brought a variety of offerings depending on what was ripe or what she'd managed to catch or dig or net on any given day. No one had ever complained and the woven baskets brimming with fresh food were always a delightful surprise.

When the Widow's baskets arrived, dinner was planned around the bounty within them, whether it was steamers and corn, wild raspberries, apples and blue crabs or lobsters, arugula and fresh scallions. Always there were flowers from early spring on; first tulips and daffodils, then iris, lupine and wild sweet peas, then the zinnias, asters, cosmos, marigolds, coreopsis, snapdragons, dahlias, cornflowers and all manner of wild flowers growing in riotous profusion in Winward's meadows.

This morning would be spent repairing her lobster traps in preparation for the following week when they would be baited and set out for the first time. She also needed to make several new baskets as she had reluctantly agreed to take on four new clients this year. Some of the old baskets were worn and split, in need of repair. Fashioned from rushes, dried in the sunroom over the winter, the baskets were strong and water-resistant, their large willow handles smooth and comfortable to hold, even when they were heavily laden with produce. Along with the baskets, she sometimes used burlap sacks for her deliveries if she was bringing large quantities of shellfish.

Each customer was allotted two baskets and several bags per season, the empty one to be returned with the following delivery. If a basket was lost or misplaced, she had begun charging for new ones. Some people feigned loss in order to have one of the simple, but beautiful baskets to take home at the end of the season so she was careful to set aside enough of the cattails and rushes for drying in order to replace worn or "misplaced" baskets. Several times customers had suggested that she might like to sell some baskets to the local gift shops or stores in the city, where they assured her she would make a handsome profit. Addie always demurred.

As she went about her afternoon chores, she began to relax. They would stay on their side and she would stay far away. She knew every inch of the island and every hiding place. Six months and they would be gone. She would find a way to bear it.

CHAPTER 4

Ned arrived in the village of Tripp's Landing in the late morning. Phil had told him to arrange transportation across the channel to Winward Island with Abe Rudder at something called the *Pickle Shack*. After asking a couple on the main street, he had been directed to the docks and Rudder's Pickle Shack, so named, he learned later, because the dilapidated building had once housed a local pickling business, *"Ma Milly's Dillies."* The building now appeared to be a boat repair business and storage facility for small craft. As Ned approached, the man himself emerged, ruddy faced and jowled, ushering Ned into a small, cluttered office alongside the warehouse.

"Winward Island? Say, you ain't headed fer the Barlow place are ya?"

"No sir, I'm camping on the SENCA conservation land. Do you know about us?"

"Nope, but then I don't go in much fer them save the earth groups and stuff. People around here been livin' that way fer centuries without no fancy names. Whatcha doin' out there anyhow, sonny?"

"A study of the animal and plant life," Fielding replied, trying to remember the last time someone had called him "sonny." "A rare burying beetle was sighted on the island last summer. Until recently, the species was thought to be extinct. Found only in a few places in the world—Block Island, and now maybe on Winward Island."

"That so. Who told ya, the Widow?"

"As a matter of fact, it was by chance. A group of college students discovered them on a canoe trip. Other than that, I don't believe anyone's been out there."

"Not if she has anything to say about it."

"Are you referring to Mrs. Barlow?"

"Yep. A witch, some folks say. Bet she's not lookin forward to yer visit. Hates people. Avoids 'em like the plague 'cept when she can't help it. Better watch yerself with her—she's a right spooky one, that."

Phil had called ahead and arranged for a boat to ferry Ned out to the island. After shaking hands, they had moved right to the task at hand, loading the equipment into Rudder's boat.

Almost a full head taller than Ned, Rudder stood gawking, his long bony arms protruding from the frayed flannel shirt. His shirt sleeves were rolled up, the skeletal arms covered in sweat and grease. In his late fifties, early sixties, the man had a youthful spring to his step, belying evidence of advancing years in his balding pate, grey scraggly beard and stooped shoulders. He wore overalls, held up by suspenders, faded to grayish black from seasons of grimy work and complaisant laundering.

His son stood behind him, silent and watchful, broad where his father was narrow. A thick head of dirty blond hair protruded from under a New York Mets baseball cap. In his late teens, the son was dressed similarly to the father in the same grey-white overalls, the letters "P.S." stitched over the top pocket. Under his overalls a white T-shirt, soaked with sweat, clung to his muscular frame.

"Mr. Rudder, what exactly do you mean, spooky?"

"Well, I won't be a tellin' no tales Mr. Fielding, but she's been livin' a long time on that island. Not quite human no more if you ask me, but you'll see fer yerself. If, that is, she ever lets you see 'er. Probly stand a better chance of seein' her here in town than you will out there. She'll expect you to keep yer distance, I'll wager."

After a number of trips to and from Ned's car, Rudder, his son, and Ned had loaded everything.

"Now, look here, Rudder."

"How you gonna git back and forth?" the elder Rudder interrupted.

"The agency is sending a canoe down next week. When it comes, I've asked your son to bring it out. Now, about Mrs. Barlow."

Ignoring Ned's question, Rudder muttered, "Don't know as he can make too many trips out there. Like I say, folks don't like to get too near."

"Dad, I already said I would. Besides, you know I don't believe all that shit about the Widow."

"Watch yer tongue boy. Git down here and help Mr. Fielding." Clearly miffed at his son's dismissal of his carefully orchestrated warnings and innuendo, Abe scowled as Rufus loaded the last of Ned's supplies into the boat and hopped in.

"Thanks, Rudder. Well, I'm off. Be in town a few times a week once the canoe arrives."

"Rufus, get back here quick boy. Good luck, Fielding! Stay on yer own side of the island!"

Waving, Ned signaled to Rufus and they shoved off. As they rounded the point, leaving the harbor behind them, Winward Island came into view, the mists of the morning parting slightly to reveal her green, rocky splendor.

"So what's your theory on Mrs. Barlow, Rufus? Do you think she's half human too?"

"Don't know," his companion mumbled, quiet now as they neared the shore.

When they reached the dock, Rufus unloaded the supplies, stacking them on the dock with lightning fast speed. The last of the gear had hardly touched the dock when he had fired up the motor and shoved off, not even pausing to say goodbye. Ned shook his head, staring morosely at the pile. He had hoped that Rufus would help carry the supplies to his campsite.

"Oh well," he said aloud. "I've got six months."

CHAPTER 5

As Ned carried the first load down the path, carefully marked on the rough map Phil had given him, he thought about his situation, his wife, his children, and his life. What a mess. He realized how fortuitous this job opportunity had been, giving him time away to forget and to plan. Perhaps his stay on the island would give him time to decide what he wanted from life.

As he had predicted, the kids wholeheartedly supported his decision. Sydney had cried, "Oh, Dad, what incredible luck for you right now! Just what you need! If I weren't so tied up here I'd be tempted to sneak out for a visit. That area's meant to be gorgeous!"

"Do you think I'm shirking my responsibilities, Syd? I mean, would you guys rather I stayed and settled things with your mother now?"

"Dad, do you hear yourself? Only one person in this family thinks that way—Mom. And you know she'll string you along for a year or two if she can get away with it. You know damn well you'd be twiddling your thumbs at home for the next six months. Please don't start thinking like her, okay? One egomaniac is enough for this family! Mom will have Martin draw up the papers just the way she wants, whether you're here or not, so please go!"

"Thanks, darling. I'll write."

"Me, too. And Daddy, we're spending Thanksgiving together. You, me, Ned and Janie? Right?"

"What about your Mom?"

"Aruba, remember? Her birthday present to herself. She's already made the reservations."

"Thanksgiving it is then. I'll call you, Syd."

"I love you Daddy."

"I love you too, darling. Don't let the campers run you ragged." They hung up and he smiled, thinking of Sydney at camp. For the fifth summer, she was working on the Vineyard at a camp for children and adults with cerebral palsy. She had started in the children's camp, but was now working with adults. They needed her strength and her compassion for what was often a backbreaking, heart wrenching, messy job. He could hardly believe that his little girl was to be a junior at Middlebury in the fall…could hardly believe she'd grown onto such a strong, independent, beautiful woman. Ned's heart swelled with pride when he thought about all she had accomplished in her twenty years of life.

Next, he had dialed Ned Junior's number and found that his son was out. Janie, his live-in girlfriend answered. "Hey Ned, how goes it?"

"Fair Janie, how are you?"

"Great, never better. Your son keeps me hoppin' though, you know him."

"Sure do. He around?"

"Nope, away 'till next week. In Phoenix with clients. You could try his cell?"

"Listen, Janie, I'm goin' away for a while. I wanted to check it out with him. See if he, if you guys needed me for anything…for the next six months."

"Six months! Where you going?"

"Winward Island up the coast near Derryville, Tripp's Landing and New Bedford."

"Beautiful country! Work or pleasure?"

"SENCA. A survey and census of the area. Uncharted territory."

"Sounds great. Hey, don't worry about us, Ned. And you know Ned'd want you to go. After all the shit that's been going on, you deserve it. I think that's one of the reasons your Ned took the job in Phoenix, to get away from Penny. She calls here screaming ten times a day when he's around. Doesn't like me, so our phone's been nice and quiet the past few days."

"I'm sorry, Janie."

"Hey, don't beat yourself up. It's not your fault. Go. Have a great time."

"Tell Ned I'll call next week, Janie. I'm not sure cell phone reception's great on the island, but I'll send you the address when I get there and a phone number where I can get messages. Got my laptop, but I'm not counting on Internet access either. Take care and give Ned my love."

Ned knew that Janie spoke for his son and thus, her words of reassurance put his mind at ease. His children were the only thing worth living for right now, he reflected, unable to shake the uncharacteristic depression that had hung over him for the past several weeks.

He had long since turned away from the cliffs and the water, and the thicket was letting up as he headed inland. Around the next bend he cleared the brush and stepped into an open field that stretched as far as the eye could see, a field just awakening from its winter sleep. The grass, only six inches high, ran in a pulsating carpet of green to the rocky cliffs at the northwest tip of the island. The ocean lay beyond, framed by the gray, granite outcroppings, a vast blue, peppered with clouds stretching to meet the horizon miles out to sea. The rocky outcropping signaled the northern edge of the island.

Heaven. Were it not for his love and concern for his children, he would gladly have died right then, in this place that lay so peacefully amidst the undulating green and infinite blue above and in front of him.

Instead of expiring, however, he dropped his load and began searching for a suitable campsite. After several hours spent examining a number of spots and weighing their advantages and disadvantages, he settled on a sheltered corner of the meadow at the top of a rise. This location afforded a view of his surroundings while providing some protection from the elements. Rainwater would run off rather than collect around the tents and there was a flat expanse wide enough to pitch both tents and store his supplies, leaving room for his stove and a cooking pit. He had brought a four-burner Coleman stove and enough fuel for six months. Occasionally, he would make a fire for warmth, but fires were discouraged on conservation lands and daily fires for cooking were out of the question.

Satisfied at his choice of campsite, he returned to the dock for another load. It took two days and countless trips along the west path before everything was unloaded, set up and stored. Sitting back after supper on the third evening, he felt at peace for the first time in many years. No screaming phone calls from Penny, no calls from colleagues trying to lure him back to teaching, no need to confront the shambles of his life as he'd had to do every minute of the past year.

It had been nearly two years since he'd quit his job, a full professorship at Greenleaf College to work for SENCA. Penny didn't speak to him for almost a month after his resignation. Pardington millions had financed the school for many years and a Pardington, even a lowly son-in-law, did not give up a full professorship. It wasn't the salary that bothered her, although Ned's had been very generous. It was the loss of prestige. The youngest full professor in the history of the college when appointed at age twenty-seven, his team of biologists was nationally recognized, all highly respected, even without the Pardington millions.

Ned Fielding had proven to be quite a surprise to his in-laws after his marriage to their daughter at the scandalous ages of eighteen and seventeen respectively. While they didn't expect him to disgrace them, they had never, in their wildest dreams, anticipated the acclaim his studies would bring the College, and the family.

While Ned's family had been well off, the Pardingtons had insisted on financing their son-in-law's education, college and graduate studies, while Penny had raised Ned and Sydney. His appointment as an assistant professor of biology was announced the day he received his doctorate. Penny and he had packed up the kids and said good-bye to their first home, an apartment in Cambridge, and returned to Greenleaf.

Once in Greenleaf, they renovated, then moved into the three-story brick house where Ned had grown up. Both his parents had passed away by that time. Nancy, Ned's sister had kept the house, but she and her husband, Wayne, were moving to California. Ned and Penny bought her half of the house. The contents were divided equally. Penny and Nancy had made all the decisions.

Ned didn't care about any of it, or at least not enough to do battle over. He didn't care if the highboy in the living room stayed or disappeared. He didn't care if the family silver went with Nancy or remained in the house where it belonged (Penny's words).

"You take care of it, darling," he told her. "You're so much better at these kinds of things than I am. Whatever you think."

He was hopeless at making the endless decisions and when, upon the rare occasion, he stuck in his oar, it was never helpful. "Perhaps Nancy should have that, Pen. After all, it was my mother's?" After a storm of protest, "Of course, darling. I hadn't thought about Sydney. Of course, whatever you say."

When Nancy finally departed, the two women were no longer speaking. At her departure, Nancy seemed to carry away not only the vestiges of their childhood, but also whatever love had been present in Ned and Penny's relationship. Their love had disappeared along with the armoires, coffee tables, silver tea sets and canopy beds. Ned saw Nancy only once before her death, on a brief visit to Santa Barbara for a convention. He always wondered at the dissolution she had left in her wake, wondered if his sister had stayed, if things might have been different.

Once settled in Greenleaf, their lives were not their own…they were now part of the vast Pardington holdings. Father and Mother Pardington insinuated themselves into every facet of their lives. As his in-laws crept in the front door, Ned slunk out the back. While the prodigal son-in-law brought them prestige, recognition and honor, he was hardly noticed most of the time, let alone missed. Until the day he disgraced the family.

"Fortunately, Mommy isn't here to bear this disgrace!" were the only words Penny spoke to him during the entire month following his resignation. Daddy, by then confined to a wheelchair, fussed and fumed, but to no avail. By that time, the Pardington mantle had already passed on, intact and formidable, to the daughter. It was his wife, not his father-in-law, who brought the family's wrath and indignation to rain down upon him. She hadn't needed her father, her mother, or any of the legend of lawyers and executives that constituted the Pardington Empire; she spoke for them all.

Despite Penny's raging threats and insults, Ned's resolve was unwavering. Even after Penny had forced the college to revoke his pension and his benefits; he remained stalwart, determined to follow his own course. Once Ned made up his mind about something, no amount of pressure could persuade him to change. Penny had recognized this unshakable resolve in her husband from the day they had met and it never ceased to enrage her. Penny Pardington Fielding was accustomed to having things her way.

Ned had money of his own, nothing like the fortune his wife had accrued, but enough. The children were well-provided for. His father-in-law's will had made them both millionaires several times over, far wealthier than their father would ever be. They constantly asked if he needed money, which he always refused. Responsible, levelheaded people, his children, and he had no doubt that they would use their fortunes well. Their financial independence and security made his decision to pursue a less lucrative career much easier.

So here he was, stretched out in a worn camp-chair, his only furniture along with a small stool, the tables set up for his equipment, and his sleeping cot. He would begin work in the morning. He had already begun taking notes about the vegetation around the camp, the various types of meadow grasses, wildflowers and other vegetation growing in profusion around his new home. In the morning, he'd make a map that divided the SENCA property into quadrants before beginning the census. One day a week was to be set aside to study the beach as the season went on. He needed to take soil samples, measure the water temperature, and record animal activity on the dunes and open water surrounding the island.

A fox slipped by for a look at the newest island resident, and whippoorwills called as the sun sank in the western sky. From his vantage point, he could just glimpse a small section of the horizon through the trees as the sun disappeared, its orange brilliance diminishing to a slender red line before it disappeared.

With the sun's departure, Ned felt a pang of loneliness, but only for an instant. In the remaining light of day, he hopped up to clean up his supper things. As he stood at the steel washbasin, rinsing and drying the few plates and utensils, he thought he spied a dark figure on the cliffs, her body silhouetted against the faintly glowing horizon. Dropping the towel, he ran toward the point. When he reached the cliffs, she had disappeared, the woodland surrounding the point hiding her instantly within its inky depths.

"Hello!" he called, into the growing darkness, assuming he had caught sight of the Widow Barlow. He received no answer save the whispering of the meadow grass, and the screech of night heron. He walked back to the camp, wondering if perhaps he had imagined seeing her. Had the mysterious Widow come, like the fox, to inspect this newcomer? Or had the solitude and stillness of the island, like an opiate to his broken spirit, caused him to hallucinate?

He fell asleep full of questions, but simultaneously content and peaceful in his new home under the stars.

CHAPTER 6

Addie didn't know Ned Fielding. If she had, she would have avoided the north-south path that afternoon. Late afternoon always found him restless, usually walking great distances to unwind and relax. At home, it was not usual for him to walk ten miles if he had the time. The smallness of the island had concerned him when he accepted the position; six months without space enough to stretch his legs would be a problem.

He had been thrilled upon discovering the long, twisting north-south path that followed the slithering, crystal-clear stream running the length of the island. The stream eventually emptied into a small pond near the cliffs at the mouth of the cove. There were two fresh water ponds on the island, this small one and a larger, deeper pond that lay completely within the Widow Barlow's domain. After studying his map, he decided that the north-south path constituted the border dividing the two adjoining properties and he would, therefore, not be trespassing if he used it.

Lost in plans for his research, which he intended to begin the next day, he failed to see her until they were nearly upon each other. The persistent, burble of the stream had muffled sounds at both points along the trail and the woman and her pet were caught off-guard as well.

"Oh, hello," he stammered. They stood, twenty yards from each other on the soft, sandy path, Addie poised slightly above him, a blaze of sunlight at her back.

Not quite as tall as Ned, she was nonetheless tall for her sex. Her height and appearance startled him. He was aware that he was staring, but felt powerless to stop himself. Her long, chestnut hair was pulled back in a braid, short wisps of hair trailing out from beneath an old baseball cap, Red Sox, he guessed, although the lettering had long since fallen away. With the sun at her back and the cap pulled down, her face was indistinguishable except for dark eyes that returned his gaze… wary, watchful eyes. She wore faded denim overalls. Slim, muscular arms held a pail of clams with one hand and stroked the large tawny animal. Her companion stood in front of her, not threatening but protective, and the woman's legs were hidden from him, but he noticed her shoes, red canvas basketball sneakers with white athletic socks scrunched above the tops of the sneakers.

"Is that?" he said finally, looking more closely at her companion. "Is that a coyote?"

"Yes, Aran. She's tame and will not harm you. If you see her in the fields, please don't be afraid."

Her voice, a deep, gentle purr, was soothing, but Ned thought he detected a trace of fear. Fear for herself or the animal? "Ned Fielding." He approached her, hand outstretched. Before he could reach her, she stepped back out of reach, her face still shrouded and indistinguishable in the shadows. "Mrs. Barlow, I presume." He smiled and dropped his hand.

"This path may be on SENCA property." Her voice quavered. "I'm sorry. It has always been the easiest way home for me. From now on, I will go around."

"Please, Mrs. Barlow, this is your home. Feel free to use the path, or any part of the SENCA refuge. From what I understand, your efforts have protected and preserved the island. I hope you and I will be friends."

"Excuse me, Mr. Fielding, I must make something clear. I live alone by choice. I ask only that my privacy be respected. I will refrain from disturbing you, if you will accord me the same courtesy."

"Of course, but, please call me Ned."

His words were lost. She had already turned away and disappeared into the brush, regaining the path some distance below. He caught a fleeting glimpse of her profile as the loose strands of hair blew away from her face and her soft, delicate features that the rough clothes and worn cap could not completely obscure.

He stood for a long while, wondering if he'd actually met his fellow islander or simply hallucinated the entire encounter. He had been told by Phil Bodington that there had once been a small number of carnivores on the island, introduced years ago to control the deer population, but he'd not yet seen one, and had assumed that the coyotes had died out with the deer. Although the coyote had been sighted in the woods of the northeast the past few years, Ned had never seen one up close, nor had he ever heard of anyone keeping one as a pet. And, Aran, she had called her animal, was bigger than any coyote he had ever imaged.

He returned to his camp, thinking about the woman. She had made it clear that he was to respect the boundaries, but he found himself wishing that he'd been sent to study the mysterious Mrs. Barlow rather than nicrophorus americanus, a one and a half-inch beetle. Chiding himself for his foolish imaginings, he vowed that he would begin the census in the morning, rain or shine.

CHAPTER 7

Wispy clouds reached fluffy white fingers, which danced in pantomime just above the horizon. The day promised to be clear and cool. Ned loved days like this one, the air so fresh and crisp he could almost taste it. He sat at the table set up beside the entrance to his equipment tent, drinking his coffee and studying the rough topographical maps that Phil had provided him. He intended to explore one area at a time and had divided the SENCA property into eight quadrants, figuring each area would require two weeks to survey. This would give him the last month to wrap up and write his report while returning to important sites, nests, colonies of insects, and unusual vegetation to observe the onset of winter dormancy. If he needed to take specimens, this last month would also be used for careful collection. Phil had said the specimen collection was not a priority unless he made a discovery that warranted further study and collaboration.

He looked around the tent, satisfied with his organizational efforts. His few reference books were neatly ensconced in a makeshift bookcase, an empty carton he had perched on the end of the dissecting table. Besides the table at which he now sat, there was a longer, sturdier dissecting table, a microscope, wooden slide box, and notebooks and drawing paper, all neatly arranged. Two folding metal chairs and a corner of the tent had been consigned to a jumble of cartons and boxes, some empty, some full, containing specimen jars, camera equipment and a small collection of tools.

Ned liked order, sadly absent at home for many years. Penny thrived on chaos and seemed to purposely create disarray, which Ned suspected was designed to keep him off-balance. His two worn canvas surplus tents pitched in the clearing already afforded him a sense of order and peace that his home never had.

He had decided to tackle the farthest quadrants first, then work his way back towards his camp as the summer progressed. With this plan in mind, he collected his equipment and packed his daypack. He took binoculars, a notebook, several field guides, collection jars, a clicker to aid his counting, a collapsible insect net, camera and film, a small spade and a handful of plastic bags. He also packed a lunch, a thermos of lemonade, and a canteen of water.

His maps showed several fresh water streams running through the refuge, but aside from the stream near his campsite and the stream running alongside the north-south path, he knew of no other fresh water sources. He had already tested the water in his stream and found it potable. At the last minute, he stuck three small plastic vials into the pack in the event that he came upon a source of fresh water and wanted to bring samples back to test.

He checked his watch. Seven-thirty, a respectable starting time for his first workday. He headed for the northern most point of SENCA land, where he intended to spend the first few days on the beach and cliffs. He would have to return many times to the beaches and costal areas over the summer to check on the birds, animals and plants living at the ocean's edge, but he wanted to conduct a brief survey of the area, adding to his data in the months ahead.

During this initial sampling, Ned discovered several osprey nests, numerous nesting areas of gulls, terns, plovers and sandpipers as well as evidence of other birds, their aeries hidden and inaccessible on the rocky cliffs. As he reached the outermost boundaries of the SENCA land, he could look west to the vast tidal marshes, haven for hundreds of birds and animals. The area was inaccessible by the beach, however, and he dared not trespass over the Widow's land to take a peek. He would have to content himself with observations made from the water, after the canoe arrived.

CHAPTER 8

During the second week of his stay, Ned made many trips around the island in the bright green canoe SENCA had shipped down to him. From the water, he observed all manner of wading birds…bitterns, herons and egrets and belted kingfishers, a frequent sight as he rounded the point. The tiny birds hovered high above the marsh, before plunging straight down when they spied a fish, then swiftly carrying their catch to safer ground. The marsh grasses enclosed him as he paddled through the narrow channels and inlets where mussels grew in profusion and blue crabs paddled lazily in the clear, blue-green water. At the water's edge, great colonies of fiddler crabs scuttled to safety, disappearing into the thousands of holes that dotted the open mud flats.

The marsh was a quiet world far removed from the crash of the open sea that bordered the other three sides of the island. The sheltered inlet was rare on a barrier island such as Winward. Most often, these barrier islands were completely surrounded by rocks and cliffs; almost never did one find a tidal marsh reaching out from such an island, but Winward's proximity at its western edge with the mainland's vast salt marshes, enabled the salt marsh to survive, protected by the surrounding landscape. Over and over, Ned found himself wishing that SENCA had been left the western half of the island, rather than the eastern end, since the west was a much richer field of study.

The end of the third week found Ned halfway through his study in quadrant 2. Occasionally, over the past weeks, he had glimpsed his fellow islander from a distance, paddling her kayak in the dawn hours, fishing or hauling her lobster pots off the west and north ends of the island, but they had no further encounters. While he paid little attention to his own whereabouts in relation to the mysterious Mrs. Barlow, he was certain that she was taking great pains to avoid him.

After his initial curiosity, he had almost forgotten the Widow. He hated to think of her as "the Widow," but everyone in the village referred to her as such and he had subconsciously fallen into the habit as well. A harsh name for such a young person, he thought, feeling a little sorry for his mysterious neighbor.

As yet, there had been no sign of the nicrophorus americanus and Ned was beginning to think that the graduate student had been mistaken, but he was enjoying himself. Thoroughly caught up in the work, he didn't mind his lack of success in locating the beetles.

He made several trips a week across the channel to the village in the canoe. Equipped with a small outboard motor, the craft had been delivered by Rufus Rudder at the end of the second week. Its arrival made life considerably easier for Ned. The third week, he had received a letter from Phil saying that a cart, for hauling gear from the dock to his campsite was on its way and would be there in two days' time. Better late than never, he thought, remembering the countless trips he had made that first day to and from camp. He arranged to have Rufus deliver it and promised to meet the boy at the dock. The cart, even disassembled, would never fit in the canoe.

When Ned met Rufus that afternoon, he found not only the cart, fully assembled and waiting for him, but a welcome surprise as well. Phil had sent a small portable refrigerator with enough propane to last for several years. Typical Phil, thought Ned, practically hugging Rufus as they unloaded it. Lack of refrigeration had already lost its charm and the prospect of hauling ice for the cooler all summer had been weighing on him of late. A space, albeit a tiny one, where he could keep a few cold drinks and some milk and dairy products was a welcome addition to his household.

"How ya getting' on sir, Mr. Fielding?"

"Great, thanks Rufus. Wanta come back and have a drink with me? Nothing cold I'm afraid, but I can offer you some lukewarm lemonade."

"No thanks, Mr. Fielding. I gotta git back. Sides, my pa'd kill me if he knew I'd been over on the island. You know how he is."

"Why? SENCA wouldn't care and I'd love a visitor."

"Not you sir, her."

"You mean Mrs. Barlow? Why, she's not gonna bother you. Just wants to be left alone, that's all."

"All the same, folks say that she's not above doing away with trespassers."

"That's rubbish, Rufus, and you know it. Did your dad tell you that?"

"Yes, I mean no, I mean, we ain't the only one's sayin' stuff like that. I mean, I don't necessarily believe all that stuff, but she is strange and all, and well, folks just think it's better to keep away from her."

"They don't seem to keep away from her fish and vegetables. Aren't they afraid she'll poison them?" A little surprised at his own defense of a complete stranger, Ned persisted, annoyed at what seemed like small town prejudice.

Did away with her husband. He'd heard that accusation many times from the grocery clerks in the village and Abe Rudder every time they met. Almost anyone in the village with whom he struck up a casual conversation had the same story, and the next generation had picked up on the nonsense. It reminded Ned of Fall River and the Lizzie Borden saga.

In addition to the rumors about her husband, Ned had also heard about the Widow's baskets and deliveries, about the "witchcraft" she employed that enabled her to reap harvests from both her garden and the sea unheard of on the mainland. He'd even heard a crazy story about her riding on the back of a shark, one of many animals she had bewitched to do her bidding.

"That's summer folk, sir. None of us natives, well almost none of us, get the Widow's deliveries. And what do summer folk know?"

"Rufus, do you hear yourself? Do you realize how crazy that sounds?"

"Maybe Mr. Fielding, sir, but?"

"And what about the market?" Ned interrupted, unable to let the subject rest. "What about the produce and fish she sells to Mr. Quince in the summer? You all eat that don't you?"

"Well, she ain't gonna tamper with that, now is she?"

He laughed, throwing up his hands and smiling down at the boy, who had one foot already in the boat, ready to make his getaway. "I give up, but by next week, I'll have a cold beer in this refrigerator Rufus, my man, and you might just want to reconsider your opinion of Mrs. Barlow. It'll be awful nice sittin' out on the cliffs, watching the sunset, a cold beer in your hand. Keep it in mind."

For a minute, the boy frowned, not sure if he should let down his guard. Mr. Fielding treated him like a man, not the boy everyone in the village acted like he still was. He was nineteen, and he wished his father and everyone else would recognize it and treat him like an adult.

A smile crept over the ruddy, tanned face. "Okay sir, thanks. Maybe, I will. That is, if the Widow don't eat you first."

Ned waved him off and turned back towards camp, pushing the cart laden with the refrigerator and supplies. The stories about the Widow Barlow were incredible, each one more fantastic than the last. Total nonsense, he told himself, but he couldn't help but wonder about the enigmatic woman living beside him. Couldn't help wondering what had driven her to live a life of such total, self-imposed isolation.

CHAPTER 9

Sleep never came easily to Addie. Even after twelve years, the nights were difficult. Always watching, always restlessly waiting for the unseen terror to overtake her. The stranger's voice still sounded in and out of her consciousness as she prepared for bed. Aran lay curled on the floor beside the bed, her position every night. Although the coyote preferred to sleep outdoors, and felt restless and vulnerable in the house, she would not desert her mistress. The wily animal could push open the doors to the outside, but she could not re-enter the cottage once outside. Therefore, she'd have no means of reaching her mistress when the other awoke screaming from the nightmares that still tormented her.

Images floated through her dreams that night, pleasant, at first, only later growing sinister and terrifying. She was back in her bedroom at her aunt and uncle's with a village girl helping her into the heavily-beaded, white dress, Belgian lace adorning both the skirt and bodice. She had wanted to wear her aunt's simple muslin gown, a perfect fit. Plain, but lovely, it had suited her. Aunt Mildred had been tall, like her niece; they wouldn't have had to alter the gown in the slightest, but King wouldn't hear of it.

Her fiancée had insisted a wedding gown be made especially for his bride and hired a woman from Boston to design and fit it. He had also hired Daisy, the village girl, to help Addie into the elaborate costume on their wedding day. As she dressed, she thought about her husband-to-be. King Barlow had been so kind and solicitous, not only to her, but to her aunt and uncle. He had courted her slowly, but with great tenderness and attention. As their wedding day drew near, he had been increasingly short-tempered, but her aunt said it was to be expected at such a time.

What if she looked ridiculously overdressed and frumpy in the hopelessly ornate gown? Would it, at least, please this man who had been so kind to all of them? She was marrying on account of his kindness, really, and to release her aunt and uncle from the burden of her continued presence in their household.

She told King Barlow that she did not love him, but he hadn't cared. "Allow me a few years, Adelaide, my darling. I will win your affection and your love."

So she had consented. Her aunt and uncle almost insisted she accept the proposal, so happy were they to have someone else take responsibility for the child they'd inherited from her long-dead parents. Addie was eighteen on her wedding day. No one had told her about men and women, about sexual relations, about anything pertaining to married life save the admonition to "Make Mr. Barlow happy, dear. He has been so kind!"

The image in the mirror gave way to fleeting memories of the ceremony, the reception and the ride home to the huge, white house on the hill. King Barlow had purchased the ornate Victorian edifice from old man Saddler and named it Windtop for the ocean breezes that tickled its gingerbread façade. The house with its widow's walk and sweeping porches that stretched out over the cliffs, resembled and enormous white hatbox. Freshly festooned with ornate gingerbread trim, its fresh coat of paint gleamed in the sunlight from its perch high above the village of Tripp's Landing. King Barlow had spent thousands, perhaps millions renovating the old house and it shone with a brilliance unmatched by the dwellings that surrounded it.

Their bedroom overlooked the cliffs. The pounding sea muffled sounds from within their private recesses, muffled the screams of a child of eighteen, her wedding night full of unspeakable cruelty and terror. The dream sequence moved forward and she saw herself in her bridal chamber as her husband locked the door behind them. Drunk, he staggered several times as he advanced towards her.

"Remove the dress, my dear. We wouldn't want anything to happen to it."

Trembling and terrified, Addie had retreated to the dressing room where she removed her shoes and veil, but the hundreds of satin covered buttons, slippery in her shaking fingers, refused to give way. There was no one to help except her husband, sprawled out on the bed awaiting her.

"Perhaps I'll just go and see if Mrs. Mendoza could help me to unfasten my dress, and I'll be right back."

"Come here. Don't be shy. Let me see what I can do."

And so she had gone to him, allowed him to unfasten her, his fingers working slowly and carefully, so as not to tear the dress. When the dress lay tenderly draped over the chair beside the bed, the tenderness ceased.

The frightened bride turned away from the bed, intending to go back to the dressing room for her nightgown of silk and lace, a wedding present from her aunt and uncle. Before she could take a step, his hands clawed at her petticoats and tore open the bodice of her slip.

"You belong to me now, Adelaide, to do with you what I will. A husband's privilege. Don't struggle. It will only make things more difficult."

Addie woke screaming, as she found herself once again reliving the brutal attack. His heaving body loomed over her, his every thrust more painful than the last. Her body felt as if it were splitting in two. The poor young bride cried out, her heart broken, the feather pillow beside her soaked with tears. As she woke and sat up, Addie found Aran licking her tear-streaked face. Even now, with her faithful friend beside her, she could hear his laughter as he rolled off and staggered out, still dressed in his wedding suit, to his room down the hallway.

Ned awoke, too, to the screams that pierced the stillness of the windless night. The breeze carried her cries over the fields, heart wrenching sounds that tore into his dreams like a brushfire. Fully awake, he shook, uncertain of what he had heard. Had it been a nighthawk or an owl screeching, or was it, as he suspected, the Widow Barlow who had cried so piteously? Although not yet light, Ned could see the dawn creeping up on the horizon and decided to get an early start on the day. There was no way he'd be able to sleep after that awakening.

An early riser by habit, he rose and began his breakfast, then set out. Destined to awake again and again with her night terrors, he never got over the sick feeling in the pit of his stomach caused by these sudden awakenings. The screams usually came just before dawn and he found, as the weeks progressed, that he woke earlier and earlier in anticipation of them.

CHAPTER 10

During first weeks on the island, Ned completed a survey of the beaches and coastal areas and made a rough survey of the SENCA property, drawing up more accurate maps than those with which he had been furnished. The north meadow where he pitched his tents was the area of his map he designated with the coordinates A-1. He had decided to start with the land furthest from his dwelling and move closer to home as the weeks went by. The initial data-gathering had gone well and he had completed one quadrant, and was currently midway through work on the area he had designated as B-3, the area just south of B-4. This land lay adjacent to the Widow's property and was bordered on the eastern side by the stream and the north-south path.

In each area, he had set out dead mice and moles, trapped near his camp, to lure the carrion beetles. Carefully screening the carrion to keep coyotes and larger animals from stealing the bait, he checked the sites daily. So far, his efforts had proven fruitless. No sign of nicrophorus americanus as of yet.

His quarry, the Giant Carrion Beetle, remain hidden by day, then engaged in a "dance macabre" at night. Guided by a keen sense of smell, it takes to the air searching for dead birds, rodents and possibly larger mammals to feed on or reproduce near. Either it was too early for the beetles' emergence, or perhaps the college students had been mistaken.

Despite his disappointment at failing to attract the beetles, he was working hard, already filling notebooks with findings and observations carefully gleaned during days spent in all weather conditions. Gathering representative specimens of grasses, plants and flowers, he dried and pressed unusual ones. Others, he examined and discarded. Unusual insect specimens—beetles, and several species of moths, already stood mounted on large boards, ready to send home at monthly intervals.

Engrossed in his work, he gave little thought to the Widow Barlow. After meeting her on the north-south path, he had spied her only twice from afar. Catching glimpses of her left him with an unshakable loneliness. Despite his curiosity, he found himself dreading the sight of her and the mood in which it invariably left him.

He enjoyed his trips to the village for food, hardware and cell phone service. In spite of their narrow-minded ways, he looked forward to the villagers' company. As Janie had predicted, when Ned finally reached his son, Ned Junior had wholeheartedly endorsed his decision to come out to the island. Even so, Ned was relieved to talk to him and felt more settled after their conversation. "Hey Dad, go for it," had been the latter's advice, and Ned had hung up with a smile.

"That yer boy you was talkin' to?" Abe Rudder had asked. "Bet you didn't tell him much about the Widow, did ya?"

"What is there to tell, Rudder? I don't know Mrs. Barlow, and it's not likely I will, so there's not much to say, is there?"

"Still, if I was you, I'd ah said somethin'. You never know what might happen with a witch around."

"Look here, Rudder."

"Abe."

"Abe." Ned leveled his voice, determined to remain cordial. "What have you got against Mrs. Barlow? Why, she's no more a witch than you or I."

"Killed her husband, didn't she?"

"Did she? Why isn't she in jail then?"

"Got off, but folks ain't stupid. They know a vixen when they see one. Killed him and went to live out there all alone with those wild creatures she's tamed."

"You mean the coyote? Why, that's not so unusual."

"Tain't just the dog. There's the eagle, or whatever it is, and the fish."

"Fish?"

"Got some giant sea monster she rides around on all summer. Scares folks that see her half to death."

"Really, Rudder. Don't tell me you believe all that. Have you seen her riding on this sea monster?"

"Nope, but plenty have. Laugh if you want Fielding, but you'll see. Just don't press yer luck."

Ned had heard similar stories from other locals. Codington at the hardware claimed to have seen her riding on the sea monster one summer evening, and Ivy Eldrich, who owned the bake shop was convinced Adelaide Barlow was a murderess, but like the others, had no proof to substantiate her claims.

One thing was evident, King Barlow had been well-loved by the villagers, generous and civic-minded. His death had cut off a substantial source of revenue for the Tripp's Landing population, and while he had willed his home to the town, all his assets had gone to SENCA, along with the western half of Winward Island.

No longer were village lads employed summers to tend the extensive grounds of Windtop. Nor were carpenters called out for the ceaseless renovations and improvements King ordered with regularity. At his death, six additional outbuildings—sheds, barns, garages and greenhouse—had been added to the grounds and there had been plans for more to come. No longer did the fat Barlow wallet open to contribute to school fundraisers, political campaigns and capital fund drives. "If it needed doing, ask the King," was an adage laid to rest with his death.

While in town, Ned always spent a few hours on his laptop, answering e-mails, sending reports and communicating with friends, family and colleagues. One day, after completing his business, he had googled King Barlow, but found little except some newspaper excerpts about his philanthropy to the village and surrounding area.

Time passed and, while he listened to the gossip, he paid it little heed. In truth, he felt a measure of pity for the lonely woman who shared his island. Still, he kept his distance out of respect for her privacy and because he did not relish the despair that enveloped him whenever he caught sight of her. However, a chance encounter, as he headed home late one warm afternoon in early May, changed his perception of Adelaide Barlow, as well as his resolve to steer clear of her.

CHAPTER 11

It had been a long day, the sun scorching on his back for twelve hours. Mid-day he took a break to meet Rufus at the dock for the mail delivery. The boy also delivered the Widow Barlow's mail, but this he dropped into a green chest at the end of the dock. Ned too had a small letter chest he'd fashioned out of an old specimen box, but he usually met Rufus at noon for a few minutes of conversation.

Rufus had been in a hurry, unable to linger for his customary fifteen or twenty minutes. Therefore, Ned found himself on the north-south path returning to work sooner than usual. A few magazines and a packet from Phil tucked under his arm, he walked slowly, reading a letter from Penny.

"Ned…

She never used 'dear' to address him in writing, even when they were 'in love'…

Will you please write or call immediately to inform me of your plans.

I cannot stand another week of this nonsense. Martin has advised me of my

rights and I insist on your returning this week so we may settle

things. I simply cannot go on like this. If I do not hear from you

directly, I will have no recourse but to appropriate everything.

Martin has said, of course, that I deserve it all, but I am willing

to be fair. However, I must hear from you right away! I will await

your arrival by the week's end.

P."

Poor Martin, Ned thought crumpling the letter and stuffing it in his knapsack. Longsuffering Martin Lawson, the Pardington's lawyer for all his life, like his father before him, had been sucked into the business right out of law school. Ned had nothing against Martin. In fact, they had been in each other's weddings and Martin was Ned Junior's godfather. Martin's ex-wife, Catherine, had once been a dear friend of Penny's. Catherine and Martin had always seemed more compatible to Ned than he and Penny, but the Lawsons had separated and divorced more than a year ago. Ned suspected that Penny had had something to do with the break-up.

Certain that the business about Penny's rights had come from his wife and not her attorney, Ned also knew that his old friend would do just what his employer wanted in the end. There was no fighting Penny when she set her mind to something. Ned resolved to write rather than call and would get something out in the mail the next day, stating for the third time that he would be home at the beginning of November. Let her take it all, the house, the silver, the furniture, everything. He always inserted an offer to take Haggardy when he wrote, knowing full-well that Penny would keep him out of spite.

Shaking thoughts of Penny from his mind, he returned to work. It was on this day of searing heat that he found his traps disturbed for the first time, not by the carrion beetles, but by some other predator who had taken the bait. He suspected the interloper might be a fox or perhaps the Widow's coyote. After several trips back and forth to the campsite, he was satisfied that the screens and barriers he had erected would foil the larger animals.

CHAPTER 12

A little after five, his usual quitting time, he began to collect his gear. With almost four hours of daylight left, he planned a long walk and a swim in the ocean before supper. If he planned it right, he would have dinner in hand in time to enjoy what promised to be a glorious sunset. The ocean was still icy cold, in the low 50's, but it would feel great after the day's heat.

Finally packed up, he was about to sling the heavy knapsack onto his back when he heard laughter nearby. Laughter was not a sound he had come to associate with his fellow island dweller, but who else could it be but the Widow? As he listened, more laughter and splashing sounds reached him.

B-2, the quadrant in which he currently worked, was bordered on the east by the north-south path that divided the two properties. Ned knew from walks taken several weeks earlier that a pond lay close to the path. He envied the Widow her pond and would have loved to avail himself of it for bathing and water. He had discovered it the previous month on a late-afternoon walk, but it was no longer visible from the path, hidden now by the new spring growth.

Remembering the coyote, he checked the wind's direction. Easterly. He was probably safe. He crossed the path and crept through the bushes, down on all fours, taking care to stay well hidden. As thorns caught his hair and scratched his face and arms, he began to feel foolish. He contemplated turning around, but curiosity won out. The laughing had now given way to sounds of swimming and splashing. All at once, he found himself at an opening in the brush and had a clear view. A large pond stretched out before him, a body of water of which he was only aware through his maps. He had never set eyes on it or had such an excellent view of her cottage, perched on the hill, a long winding path leading from the house to the pond.

His hiding place, on the slight rise, afforded him a view of the easterly half of the island he had never seen. On his canoe trips around the island, trees shielded this area from view. Ned felt as if he had stumbled upon a secret garden, a magical, otherworldly place. He would have liked to stand, for a better view. To the north and west of the house, gardens were already in bloom with early flowers and vegetables. These gardens stretched down almost to the pond, where watercress had been carefully cultivated.

A scream of delight called his attention back to the pond and he turned just in time to see a splash. Seconds later, a head bobbed up with its back to him, at the northeast corner. A small stream emptied into the water here, and an eight-foot waterfall flowed over moss-covered rocks into the swirling pool below. She treaded water, beckoning to the coyote, which now stood near the top of the cascade.

"Come on, Aran! You can do it! What a baby you are!"

The animal inched towards the water, putting one paw in, then withdrawing it. Finally, she gave up, and began threading her way along the stream to the pond's edge. Then, she turned and swam vigorously away from the stream, strong arms slicing through the glassy water. Seeing his mistress' retreat, the coyote leaped onto the slippery rocks to be carried, paws flailing, into the depths below.

Hearing the splash, she reversed direction and was at the animal's side in seconds. "You did it, my brave princess!" She laughed and held the coyote long enough for the animal to regain her composure and begin to swim alongside her.

Ned brushed beads of sweat from his forehead and eyes, the gesture momentarily blocking his vision. Even in the shade, the heat was oppressive, and his hiding place was like an oven. He wished he could join the frolicking pair, but he dared not move, scarcely dared breathe as they swam towards him. As they swam past, veering towards the path on the opposite side of the island, he recognized that he had intruded on a private moment he had no right to share. Despite his curiosity, he began to feel guilty for intruding, then frightened and embarrassed. Who was he to spy on this woman who had asked to be left alone? She had shared her island gracefully, if reluctantly, and now here he was, no better than a peeping Tom.

He dared not move, lest the woman or the animal discover him, so he sat watching and listening as they swam past and headed for the water's edge. His legs were cramping up and his knees ached painfully from an old football injury. He longed to stand and stretch. Then, as the Widow Barlow emerged from the water, Ned Fielding forgot his aching knees and cramped thighs as he gazed with awe and wonder at the sight before him.

The far edge of pond seemed suddenly closer and he imagined that he could almost reach out to touch her. Her shimmering nakedness took away what little breath he dared to draw. He clamped his hand over his mouth, fearful that an involuntary cry might escape. Had he cried out? Neither woman nor coyote had turned, so he assumed that his had been a silent wail, emanating from some primal source deep within.

While she swam, Ned had had difficulty making out the woman's features, obscured by the glare on the water and the splashing of her pet beside her. Now, although she had her back to him, as her long graceful form rose from the glassy water, her beauty was revealed in startling clarity.

Strong shoulders tapered to a delicate waist and smooth, rounded buttocks, curving to long slender legs. Her long brown hair fell almost to her waist. She held it back as she stooped to retrieve a towel in the grass. Ned covered his eyes at this juncture, out of shame, remorse or wonder, he wasn't quite sure, but when he uncovered them, she had turned full around and faced him now, calling to her pet. It was no longer possible for him to look away. The late afternoon golden sun kissed her glorious body, still wet from the swim. Ned was awestruck.

He had seen few naked women in his thirty-eight years, but how different the creature before him was from his wife. Although lovely, Penny now seemed emaciated and sickly by comparison. Her regimen of dieting and aerobics kept her figure skeletal. When he held Penny in his arms, his fingers fit comfortably between her ribs, even through her layers of clothes. How would it be to hold this glorious creature, her strong body full of curves? Her, round, full breasts, tanned and firm, glistened with wetness as she fastened the towel around her waist and collected the rest of her things from the grass. Long graceful hands smoothed strands of hair from her face as she gathered the chestnut tresses behind her, making a half-hearted attempt to dry them with another towel.

On their brief encounters, her face had always been well hidden by the baseball cap, its brow pulled down low. Now, as she looked skyward, its haunting beauty was revealed and his heart was pierced with sudden sadness. Hers was a handsome face, browned by the sun and chafed by the wind, but when she lifted her chin, her features softened and looked almost delicate.

As he watched, transfixed, no longer the slightest bit concerned about the heat or his previous discomfort, a sound emanated from deep in her chest. He imagined he could almost see the sound warbling up her long, slender neck, before it burst from her lips into the air. A whistle, but an unusual one, almost like the call of an exotic bird strayed from paradise.

She continued whistling and scanning the skies for several minutes before sadly turning away. As she turned away, Ned thought he spied a tear glistening on the smooth, high cheek, but he couldn't be sure, just as he couldn't be certain of the color of her dark eyes, far away and yet clearly filled with sorrow.

As she and the coyote made their way up the path towards the cottage, he felt his own heart contract and a wrenching sadness of separation washed over him. He wanted to stand and cry out, "Wait for me!" but that would be foolish and unwise. After all, he was an interloper, a lecherous spy, unwelcome in this sacred place. After they disappeared into the cottage, he rose and crawled on all fours until he reached the path. Near to tears and suddenly, desperately tired, he gathered his things and headed back to camp.

After a long frenzied walk, a very cold swim and a dinner that he scarcely tasted, he found himself sitting in the cool of the evening thinking about her. From that day on, the SENCA work became secondary for Ned. He continued to survey, his methods meticulous and thorough, but his heart was not longer in the work. Instead, a good portion of every day, was devoted to a more engrossing subject, the Widow Barlow.

Despite his efforts to spot her, the woman remained elusive. His tracking methods, primitive and tentative at best, allowed her to keep considerable distance between herself and her pursuer. On several occasions, he returned to his hiding place by the pond, but the swimmers never appeared. He began to suspect she had discovered his presence and he felt ashamed and angry.

Despondent and lonely, he finally decided that he must make contact. To this end, he began leaving notes in her letterbox, inviting her to dinner. The notes were dropped, unopened, into his own letter box until finally, after numerous attempts, he gave up, resigned to never meeting or seeing her again.

After hours of chastising himself for acting like a fool, he threw himself into his work with renewed fervor. While there were still no signs of the carrion beetles, he collected a number of other rare, perfect specimens, butterflies and smaller insects. He filled many notebooks with data that would prove invaluable to future SENCA studies on the island.

His would be the only in-depth study, but the island would prove a rich laboratory for students in small field groups. Phil was talking about coming out in August with a couple of his teaching assistants. He was calling it a field study, but Ned knew Phil just wanted a break from the office, the phones and his continual fundraising activities. He found himself looking forward to the visit and wished time would move faster.

It was already early July. He was making excellent progress, but was no longer content or happy. Restless and lonely, her sad beautiful eyes haunted his every waking moment, and his dreams as well. Often, he woke in the middle of the night, her screams piercing the stillness. He no longer mistook them for the wind or his own nightmares, as they often came when he was fully awake, in the hours just before dawn. Her cries distressed him and left him in a fevered, agitated state for days afterward. He fretted about her safety, yet knew he was powerless to help.

As July sailed along, the blue skies and warm weather lifted his spirits and chased some of the worry and anxiety away. Slowly, he began to enjoy the island again, as he had upon his arrival and thoughts of his mysterious neighbor occupied his mind less frequently. As Ned settled down to work, a measure of peace returned.

Chapter 13

Monday morning dawned clear and mild, the winds blowing in gentle gusts as Ned paddled across the channel to the village. It had been over a week since he'd made the trip and almost all his provisions were depleted. He paddled out of necessity, as the canoe's motor was at Abe Rudder's for repairs. The water was choppy, but the canoe sliced through the waves and he made good progress. He hoped the motor would be ready. He didn't relish the thought of paddling the heavily loaded-canoe against the tide on his return trip.

As was his custom, he had risen early and worked in the field until almost noon. Then, he gathered his things and set off for the dock. Leaving the cove behind, he turned to look back at the island. It was a habit acquired years earlier. When leaving home, he always looked back, to take one last look. Despite clear skies, the eastern side of the island appeared to be shrouded in mist, the trees barely discernible at the edge of the cliffs. His side of the island, the SENCA property stood in sharp contrast, the sun illuminating every tree, every bush in a profusion of summer greenery. The cliffs were awash in color with the purples and pinks of the wild sweet peas and blazing yellow silverweed that crept over the grey granite outcroppings. His eyes scanned the cliffs and tree line, hoping for a glimpse of her. Finally, he turned away and paddled for the village with strong, steady strokes.

He arrived just after one and headed for Elsie's Diner for lunch. The lunch crowd had thinned and he sat alone at the counter, rechecking his lists and planning his afternoon shopping. Abe Rudder and two other men sat at a booth nearby, chatting. They had long finished lunch, but appeared in no hurry to get back to work.

"Fielding! Didn't expect to see you today, what with the storm and all."

"Hey, Abe. Yup, I'm out of everything. Had to brave the trip. Besides, the radio this morning said it wasn't expected to amount to much."

"Latest reports I hear say to expect a bad one. Tain't that so, Charlie?"

His companion, Charlie Danielson, the owner of the only drug store in the village, nodded. "S'posed to be quite a blow."

"You're a dang fool, anyway, Fielding," Abe interrupted, "You shouldn't be rowin' around in that pea pod of a thing with any kind of wind. The channel gets rough with a 30 knot breeze, never mind when the winds really pick up."

"I'll be fine." He smiled, turning to give Elsie his order.

After placing his order, Ned stuck his lists in his pocket and braced himself for the usual onslaught of questions about the Widow Barlow and his research.

"A she-devil, that one is. Steer clear of her if you know what's good fer ya."

"Come on Charlie, she ain't that bad." Jack Turner piped up from a booth in the corner. Turner, a former lawyer who'd handled some of King Barlow's affairs before his retirement, was one of the few people Ned had ever heard defend Mrs. Barlow. "What's Addie Barlow ever done to you? And her aunt and uncle were great people."

"Jack, you've gone soft in the head since yer retirement. Why you even said yerself at the time that you thought she was guilty."

"Now Abe, you know that's not so. I had words put in my mouth. By the coroner, by the police, and even by some of my good friends. Far as I'm concerned, Addie was acquitted and that's that."

"How did Mr. Barlow die?" Ned asked. All he'd ever heard was that his wife had killed him. The charge sounded so preposterous that he'd never bothered to inquire further, but perhaps Jack Turner would provide an unembellished account.

"Heart attack." Turner replied, before the others had time to speak. "King had a heart condition for a number of years. High blood pressure, overweight, the usual, and he took terrible care of himself besides."

"Don't you believe it, Fielding. He was driven to it. Young wife and her constant demands. You know, the physical business 'twas just too much for the King. He tried as long as he could, then his poor heart just up and quit."

"Your right about one thing, Abe." Jack said. "That's exactly what happened. His heart just quit. Natural causes, that's called. And that's what the coroner called it, too."

"Let's not forget how he was found. Stretched out, stark naked on the bed. They'd been, you know…folks said there'd been plenty of time fer her to get his medication. Right there in the dressing room, not ten feet away, it was. She knew what she was doin' same as if she'd held a gun to his head. Had his attack and she just sat there and watched him go."

"Now Abe, that's flat out ridiculous and you damn well know it!" Jack Turner had risen now, his face flushed. To Ned, the man almost looked as if he were on the verge of tears.

"Did to! Old Sally twere there. She knew the story. The doc said there'd have been plenty of time. That woman let her husband die sure as I'm sittin' here!" Abe had risen too, arms akimbo, ready for battle.

Charlie turned to Ned, "No one'll ever know, Mr. Fielding, but folks sure miss King. He was awful good to Tripp's Landing. Ain't gonna never see the likes of him again. No one much cares for the Widow 'cause they think she took away a lot of folks' livelihood when she let him die. P'rhaps she couldn't have saved him."

"She sure didn't try!" Abe stormed out of the diner. Over his shoulder, he called, "Motor's ready, Fielding. You can pick it up anytime. I'd get yer provisions and head out quick. Better yet, let Rufus bring things over tomorrow and head out now."

"Thanks, Abe. I'll be as quick as I can."

He settled up with Elsie and bid a hasty good-bye to Charlie and Jack. As he rushed from store to store, the village was abuzz with predictions about the storm. "Gonna be a big one," seemed to be the prevailing assessment. As the wind picked up, Ned began to feel twinges of trepidation about the return trip. His fears were not allayed when he arrived back at the docks. Abe and Rufus were busy hauling small dories, securing moored sailboats and battening down the craft tied up at the docks. "Fielding, 'bout time you showed up!" Abe called from the deck of a cabin cruiser. "'S'pose you'll be wantin' our extra bed tonight. No bother. Yer welcome to it!"

"Thanks, Abe, but if you'll get me the motor, I'll load up and shove off."

"Not a good idea, Mr. Fielding," Rufus called. "You'll get caught in the channel for sure and the current's a bitch. Tide's goin' out so it'll be pullin' hard."

"I'll be fine, really, but I'd like to get started. Can I get the motor myself? I don't want to take you away from your work."

After ten minutes of wrangling, the Rudders finally helped him load up. With repeated threats to call the harbormaster, Abe finally succeeded in persuading Ned to leave all but the food he needed that night, promising that Rufus would bring the rest out first thing the next day. Acquiescing, Ned took enough food for his supper and left the rest.

"You're crazy, you know it? Better radio over when you get there so we won't worry all night."

"Thanks, Abe. See you tomorrow, Rufus."

He shoved off and, starting the motor as he cleared the dock, headed out of the harbor into the narrow channel that separated Winward Island from the mainland. It was less than half a mile across the channel and he figured he'd be home in plenty of time to watch the storm come up the coast, a cold beer in hand.

CHAPTER 14

It was choppy and rough, but he reached the Point of Rocks, the opening of the harbor, in good time. Since the wind blew from the southeast, he had been protected by the point while still in the harbor. Once he rounded the headland, however, things became a bit livelier. Most days a meandering current ran through Cooper's Channel, strong but manageable. Today, he was greeted by a rolling mass of whirlpools, eddies and swirling fury. He contemplated turning back, but knew the ribbing and "I told you so's" that awaited him. Steeling himself, he cranked up the motor and pressed onward. It would take a while, but he'd make it. The island was so close.

Almost immediately, the canoe lurched and began to follow the current westward towards the open sea. "Shit," he cried, to the wall of wind that had risen out of nowhere. A deafening roar pierced his eardrums and deadened all sensation save the vibrating outboard tiller, which he struggled to hold steady. With great effort, he straightened the tiller, endeavoring to steer across the current.

For a while, he seemed to make slow, but steady progress. Several times, the light craft spun completely around and skipped over the waves. Each time, he recovered and steered the canoe back on its course, encouraging himself and the now-sputtering engine with mumbled prayers and whispered praise. A strong swimmer, he recognized he would be helpless should the craft capsize; there would be no swimming in this. He would be sucked under immediately.

Almost midway across the channel, the unthinkable occurred. After several minutes of coughing and spitting, the motor sputtered and went silent. No amount of coaxing and swearing would induce it to start up again. By the time he looked up from his exertions, the island was lost from sight. He found himself far out into the open sea, land no longer visible on either side.

Trying not to panic, he surveyed the situation. If he hoped to make any headway with paddling, he realized that the canoe would have to be emptied. As he tossed over the two bags of groceries and a small tackle box, he noticed an alarming amount of water in the canoe's bottom. Each crashing wave brought more water, adding to the weight and Ned's frustration. Despite frantic bailing, he couldn't possibly keep the tiny craft afloat against such an onslaught. The useless motor would have to go, he realized that. He'd have to deal with Phil's wrath at its loss, that is, in the unlikely event that he survived.

He fought his way to the stern and crouched, half standing, half kneeling to reach the clamps holding the outboard. As he grappled with the bolts, tightened just a short time ago by Rufus Rudder, "nice and tight, Mr. Fielding," he dared not look around, so swiftly was the current carrying him further and further out. He had just succeeded in loosening one of the bolts when a wave struck and knocked him off balance, throwing him backward. As he fell, his head hit the side of the canoe. This is it, he thought, losing consciousness. The blackness of death closed in, blocking the sounds of raging wind and splashing waves.

CHAPTER 15

Warm rosy light filled his head and Ned wondered if he was dreaming or if the amber glow was death, comforting and peaceful. He had never seen such vivid, pulsing colors. He smiled and gave himself over to the soothing rhythms of pulsing light.

Suddenly, the dream changed and he was in the water, tossed by the waves. He hated the cold wetness and tried desperately to bring back the rosy light. Strong arms held him aloft. His head wanted so desperately to sink beneath the waves, but the mermaid wouldn't let it. She held his chin gently in her hand, her arm holding fast to his chest. He wanted so desperately to feel the rose warmth again, but he felt safe in her arms as she swam, remarkably fast, against the current. He was so desperately cold, the icy wetness piercing his skin as slivers of pain racked through his body. Tired and spent from his exertions, he gave up and all was blackness again. He dreamed no more.

CHAPTER 16

A whippoorwill's call roused him from a deep sleep. A familiar early morning sound, Ned recognized it as his whippoorwill, the one that woke him every morning. Was he home, in his tent and the storm had been nothing but a terrible nightmare? He remained still with his eyes closed for some time, listening, enjoying the warmth of the sleeping bag against the early morning chill. Pulling the covers higher, however, he sensed something was wrong. Instead of the smooth feel of his blue, nylon bag, his face brushed against wool. Soft wool, but wool nonetheless. Except for an old sweater, Ned had nothing wooly with him and the sweater had remained packed away at the bottom of his trunk.

Opening his eyes, he found himself staring at a whitewashed ceiling of pine instead of the beige mildewed roof of his tent. Sitting bolt upright, he found himself in a bedroom, sunlight pouring in from windows facing east, west and south. The walls were whitewashed and adorned with several shaker peg racks and three striking watercolors of the island. In addition to the bed, a plain pine four-poster, the room held a dresser, also of pine, a chair and table. One wall was lined with bookshelves, mostly novels, a number of mysteries and a small, but respectable selection of poetry.

His first thought was that he had been rescued by someone in the village and brought to their home, but then he remembered the whippoorwill. Surely there were whippoorwills in the countryside around the village, but the morning sounds seemed too familiar, too personal to be from someplace other than Winward. He tried to rise, but his head pounded violently at the effort and forced him to drop back onto the soft pillows. The bedside table held nothing but a glass of water. He wondered if it had been cleared for his use. He was just peeking into the drawer when he heard footsteps and the bedroom door opened softly.

CHAPTER 17

Eyes shut, Ned feigned sleep as she approached and leaned over the bed, her hand lightly touching his forehead. Jasmine, mingled with the sweet smell of the outdoors filled his senses. As she drew back, he opened his eyes, but she had turned away to frown at the untouched glass of water on the bedside table.

Dressed in a plain blue sundress, her hair was pulled back and trailed loosely down her back. Barefoot, her step was light, almost soundless. Familiarity with every inch of her home enabled her to avoid creaky floorboards. He almost wished he could go on pretending to sleep so as to catch glimpses of her as she went about her daily routines. As it was, any second she would turn, and he had not the faintest idea what he would say to the mysterious, beautiful Mrs. Barlow.

She turned and their eyes met. Hers, deep, grey blue and inscrutable held Ned's gaze, his light, hazel eyes registering dismay. Her hand shook and drops of water from the glass fell down the front of her skirt.

"You're awake."

"Yes, thank you."

Ned made a half-hearted attempt to sit up, but his head pounded so violently that he winced, crying out in pain as he sunk back down. This seemed to embolden her, and she stepped forward.

"Here, don't try to sit up. You've have a concussion, quite a bad one, I expect. I was going to take you to the mainland in a few hours if you didn't wake up. I'm sorry you had to end up here, rather than there last night, but the storm would not allow safe passage."

"Please don't apologize. Mrs. Barlow, I'm quite sure you saved my life. I'm the one who should apologize for putting you in danger. And, I can assure you, I'd much rather be lying here than in Abe Rudder's spare room."

He thought he detected a hint of a smile at the mention of Abe Rudder.

"You should be in the hospital. You must go over and have an X-ray at least."

"I'll be fine, don't worry. I've been knocked out before and lived to tell the tale."

"Do you feel like eating something? Or drinking?"

He attempted to rise again.

"Actually, I am hungry, but I don't want to put you out. If I load up with aspirin, I can make it back home. Jesus Christ."

The pain shot down his back and sent shock waves to his toes.

"Please lie back. I'll be back soon."

Five minutes later, she reappeared with a tray, on which sat a basket of warm blueberry muffins, a small dish of sliced, fresh peaches and a pot of tea. She placed the things on the night table and drew back.

"Wait, please don't go."

She nodded and sat in a wicker chair by the window.

He blushed. "I'm sorry. That sounded like a petulant child. Not sick enough to warrant supervision, but bored and wanting attention. I don't want to keep you from your work, it's just you see—"

"Mr. Fielding, there's no need to apologize. I do have work to do, but am happy to sit a few minutes. I expect you're wondering how you got here?"

"Yes, as a matter of fact."

"We saw you from the cliffs. Actually Gwydyon spotted you and alerted us. I believe you still had the use of your motor at that point. By the time we reached the cliffs, you had lost your battle with the current. We could see it was hopeless, so we set out to help you."

"But, how did you possibly manage to reach me? I mean, by that time, I was way out in the ocean."

"Branwen is a fast swimmer."

"Branwen?"

She laughed. "You wouldn't believe me if I told you. Let's just say, I had help in my rescue efforts. We've helped others before."

Her voice trailed off and her eyes clouded over, the sadness in their soft depths almost palpable. A few minutes later, she shrugged and smiled, mischief replacing the sadness.

"I'm sure you've been warned about me. I'm a witch, didn't you know?"

She spoke with her hands, the slender arms gesturing gracefully. Ned felt an overwhelming urge to grasp hold of her and run his hands up and down her smooth, brown skin.

Stop it, he told himself, feeling foolish. He'd never felt like this about anyone, not even Penny in their early days. This woman who sat regarding him with a puzzled expression was a complete and total stranger. He had absolutely no explanation for the wild fantasies he entertained every time he laid eyes on her.

"Mr. Fielding?"

Grinning, he said, "Well, there have been a few stories, but you don't exactly help your cause any."

"What would you have me do?"

"Well, for a start, it doesn't hurt to say hello."

"There would be no sense in that, Mr. Fielding. No one would respond, believe me. I'm a murderess, a witch, and an evil enchantress. Only the foolhardy would dare return my greeting. Now, if you'll excuse me, I have things to do. Enjoy your breakfast."

CHAPTER 18

He spent the remainder of the day in restless solitude. She came and cleared away the tea things without a word, after which he heard a door slam at the far end of the house. As the day wore on, his head began to clear and he found sitting up less painful. Several hours after his tea, the need for a bathroom made itself known, and he slowly pulled himself out of bed.

The floorboards creaked the instant he stepped down and he marveled at his hostess' ability to walk over them soundlessly. Taking a few steps, the room swam before him and he flailed out, certain that he would crash to the floor. He managed to grab hold of the door handle and steadied himself. He shut his eyes and breathed deeply. That's better. Come on Fielding, you can do it.

Inching slowly, he stepped out into a long hallway with small oval braided rugs thrown down at intervals along the entire length. The stairway appeared to his right and to his left another bedroom, its door slightly ajar. He felt sure it was hers, but while he would have loved to peek in, he dared not risk passing out across the threshold, to be discovered trespassing.

He hugged the wall, continuing slowly and was relieved to discover that the next doorway led to the bathroom. It was a plain, sunny room. The light, similar to the room in which he was staying, came from a long rectangular window at its far end. The walls, like those in the bedroom, were white, adorned with several small frames containing pressed wildflowers. Fluffy blue towels hung on the towel bars with more neatly folded on top of a white wicker hamper. Shaving implements and a new toothbrush lay atop a small white dresser beside the sink.

For a moment, Ned forgot his pressing need for the bathroom and advanced to the window, gazing out at the view of the gardens and pond to the west of the cottage. Marveling at the garden's symmetrical rows, green and lush in full summer bloom, he searched for his hostess, but she was nowhere in sight. As he turned away, something in the distance caught his eye and he realized with surprise that the top of his tent was visible. She could see him, but for some reason, he was unable to see the cottage from his camp.

As the afternoon sun sank lower, he dozed off and wondered how he would ever make it back to camp. When he woke again, it was dusk, and she stood before his bed with a tray. Delicious aromas filled the room from the covered dishes she held aloft.

"How are you feeling?"

"Much better."

He smiled wanly and sat up. It was true. He really did feel better.

"I have some supper. Do you feel up to it?"

"Yes, please, but won't you share it with me?"

"I've already eaten, but I will keep you company if you like."

She set down the tray and helped plump up his pillows.

Ned blushed at her closeness as she set the tray on his lap and removed the glass of ice water, placing it on the night table. She then uncovered a warm plate of fish, new potatoes and a savory mash of parsnips and carrots. A small earthenware bowl held a crisp salad of multi hued greens, adorned with bright orange nasturtium blossoms and a light vinaigrette.

"Thank you."

Once again, she took a seat on the wicker chair.

The sole, lightly poached in herbs and wine, was moist and perfectly complimented by the parsley potatoes and the vegetable mélange.

"This is incredible." An understatement. It was one of the best meals he had ever eaten. "I'm afraid I don't feed myself very well. One pot boil 'em up meals and a little bread and cheese define the extent of my culinary repertoire. I haven't had vegetables, except from a can, for months. These are amazing."

She nodded, but remained silent.

"Are they from your garden?"

"Yes, and the root cellar. The parsnips winter over very well."

"I envy you your garden. I love gardening."

His voice trailed off as he remembered Penny's endless complaints about the time he spent in his garden. After their first year in the house, she had insisted his vegetable garden be turned over to Gus Gunney, the Pardington's gardener. She instructed Gus to lay in new sod and a few "attractive perennials." When Ned had objected, Penny replied, "We simply can't have all those weeds and rotting heads of lettuce when we use the terraces for entertaining. It's an unseemly mess and I won't have it. Besides, Daddy says the grocer has better produce than we could ever grow. Only poor people garden. That's what Daddy says." And so Ned's garden, of which he had been so proud, had gone the way of almost everything that interested or involved him at home. Everything had gone, except his children.

"Mr. Fielding? Are you all right?"

Embarrassed, he realized that his hostess had been talking. "Oh, I'm sorry. Just thinking. Ancient history. I'm often accused of being absentminded, I'm afraid."

"I was just saying about the boat. Your canoe, I mean."

"I'm sorry?"

"It's lost, I'm afraid. We couldn't save it. Perhaps it will turn up along the coast."

"Oh, shit." He sat up and set the tray aside. "Abe and Rufus Rudder, they will have tried to contact me."

"Don't worry. I got word to them today…that you are safe, I mean. I also told them you'd need a lift tomorrow, to the mainland, to the hospital. You really should have that head looked at. I've arranged for them to collect you at the dock at eleven."

"How did you, I mean…"

"I do talk to some people. How do you suppose I obtain provisions, by magic?"

"That's not what I meant, I mean."

"No need to worry, Mr. Fielding. It's all settled."

"Please, call me Ned."

"I prefer Mr. Fielding, if you don't mind."

She smiled and removed the tray, not waiting for him to reply that "yes, he did mind."

She returned a few minutes later with a bowl of raspberries with three delicate lace cookies on the plate beside them, but departed quickly without a word. When she returned, to clear away the dessert dishes, she drew the curtains. She wore a long, baggy sweater against the evening chill, but the slender curves of her body were clearly discernible as she moved. Her hair, untied, fell loosely down her back, the light just catching its shining sable softness.

When she turned, she caught him staring and Ned blushed. Averting his eyes, he heard her whisper, "good night," as she closed the door.

CHAPTER 19

Screams pierced the stillness. Throwing back the blankets, Ned sat up, heart pounding. For a second, he supposed himself in the midst of a nightmare, but then she cried out again. The anguished scream of pain and terror struck to his core and he sprang up on wobbly legs and fumbled for the light. These were the familiar cries he had heard so many nights on the island. The cries for help that rang out just before dawn.

Ned staggered out of his room and managed to find a light switch in the hall. Groping his way along, he came to the door of her room. The cries guided him towards the bed and, as he drew nearer, she quieted, soft moans and sobs replacing her screams. Her body, stiff and rigid, lay close to the edge of the bed. He touched her arm and found her drenched in sweat. A low growl, growing in intensity, came from the opposite side of the bed. Too late, he remembered the coyote.

Fighting the urge to spring back and flee, he slowly stepped back, murmuring softly, "There, there, it's all right."

He wasn't sure if he spoke to the animal or the woman, but it seemed to work. The animal relaxed and the growls ceased, as did her sobs. Assured that the crisis had passed, he backed slowly out of the room. In his own bed again, sleep eluded him. The mournful cries of his strange, beautiful hostess echoed in his mind. For the first time in many years, Ned felt like crying. He finally drifted off at dawn, the melancholy veil lifting with the first rays of the rising sun.

CHAPTER 20

"Good morning."

She stood over him, a tray balanced on her hip.

"You're a late sleeper, Mr. Fielding."

Ned rose up on one elbow and wiped sleep from his eyes. "What time is it?"

His head no longer pounded with every movement and he found he could sit up without the room beginning to spin. Self-conscious, he pulled up the bedclothes.

How lovely she was, he thought, gazing up at her. Not what one would call a "classic beauty," she was handsome and when she smiled, the sharp angles of her face softened and her sad eyes twinkled with warmth.

"It's nearly ten. Remember, they're coming to collect you at eleven? I didn't want to wake you when you needed rest to recover, but you might want to start to get ready?"

"Of course. If I might have my clothes? I mean, please, if they're dry?"

"They are, but I thought perhaps a bath? I mean, since you don't have any facilities?"

Ned laughed, raising his hand. "No need to say more. I'd love a shower, and am quite sure I need one. I'll be quick. Ready in twenty minutes."

"No need to move too quickly. We'll give you a ride to the dock. Quarter to eleven will be plenty of time."

"Ride?"

She smiled. "Your clothes are in the bathroom. I'll be in the garden if you need help."

She closed the door behind her, leaving him with more questions than ever. He thought he detected a touch of irony in her voice, but she disappeared before he could question her. Ride? "Humph," he said aloud. "Perfectly capable of walking."

He wolfed down his breakfast and took a mug of hot tea to the bathroom where he again found a pot of shaving cream and a razor laid out on a towel by the sink. He sipped his tea slowly while he shaved, thinking about the mysterious Mrs. Barlow. Who was she? What had her life been like? Had she really murdered the beloved King Barlow as the villagers maintained? Or was she the victim of a brutal husband and now the fodder for small town, petty gossip? He tended to believe the latter, but perhaps his perceptions were colored by his attraction and interest in the enigmatic Widow Barlow.

When he had woken the previous day, he had been wearing his own underwear. Clean, dry underwear. Unless he was very much mistaken, this meant she had undressed and dressed him, touching him, brushing against him as she struggled with his clothes. The thought both embarrassed and aroused him.

It had been a long time since he felt the kind of stirrings for a woman that he was feeling. Even in his dazed, weakened condition, his heart raced the minute he caught sight of her. She was lovely, yes, but it was not her physical beauty that attracted him. Penny was quite beautiful. There was something else, a haunted lonely quality that drew him to her. Perhaps they were more alike than he knew? If her night terrors were any indication, she was an unhappy and deeply troubled woman. Ned resolved that, no matter what it took, he would get to know her. Clearly, this would not be easy. Despite her hospitality and help, he was sure that once they parted at the dock, the wall would go up again. He would not be invited back to the cottage on the hill.

By the time he had showered and dressed, he felt lightheaded and dizzy. When she came to fetch him, he sat, gripping the sides of the bed, bathed in a cold sweat. His head ached and he had been unable to find aspirin in the bathroom.

"Not quite back to normal yet."

He grinned sheepishly, as she came to his side, concern in her gaze.

"You've been up too long. Do you think you can make it downstairs?"

He nodded, afraid if he spoke he might lose his breakfast.

"Come, lean on me."

She helped him to stand, her strong arm supporting his back as they started down. He could feel the softness of her breast as she leaned against him and her nearness brought a mixture of comfort, arousal, and the distressing worry that he might faint in her arms and send them both hurtling down the steep staircase.

Finally, they reached the bottom step and crossed the living room. In his weakened state, he noticed little of his surroundings, save the massive fieldstone fireplace at the room's far end. Outside, a cart hitched to a large garden tractor awaited them. She helped him in.

"There you are."

She had lined the cart with two large canvas pillows, one for him to sit on, and the other for his back.

"Just lie back and we'll have you there in no time."

Ned settled back, gazing upward as they went along. Fleecy clouds passed over the infinite blue above them. A warm, almost windless day, the heat bore down as they made their way through the thicket. Sometimes he looked forward to watch her driving the tractor, but mostly he gave himself over to the blue of the sky and the sights and sounds of the woods around him.

True to her word, they reached the dock in no time. Rufus Rudder had just pulled up when they emerged from the clearing at the cliff's edge. He watched in amazement as she helped Ned from the cart, the patient leaning heavily on her as they made their way down the dock. As they neared him, Rufus ventured forth to take over, almost carrying the limp Ned to the boat. Together, they lifted him in, gently settling him in the bow.

As they withdrew, he revived. "Mrs. Barlow," he cried, in a desperate voice that he hardly recognized as his own.

She had already jumped from the boat, but turned back, regarding him.

"Thank you, thank you so very much, for everything."

She nodded and turned away. The men watched as she started the tractor and disappeared into the thicket, leaving Rufus in a state of shock and Ned feeling sick, lonely and miserable.

Finally, breaking out of his reverie, Rufus started the motor and they set off without a word.

CHAPTER 21

Severe concussion was the diagnosis. Three days in the hospital, the prescribed treatment. After the first day, Ned felt almost his old self again, except for a nagging headache, but was encouraged to stay. The village's tiny hospital, Barlow Memorial, was more like a rest home. All serious cases were sent immediately to Fall River, New Bedford, Providence or Boston. Barlow admissions and discharges were informal. If they had needed his bed, Ned felt sure he would have been discharged after a brief observation. Since things were slow, he had been welcomed to stay and rest up.

Tired and discouraged, with little desire to rush back to his research, Ned accepted the invitation without a whimper to the doctor's recommendations. He called the local bookshop and had them send over a stack of mysteries, then settled back and enjoyed hot meals, cooked up by Elsie in the diner's kitchen and sent over three times a day.

The first day, Phil visited and brought another canoe and outboard motor. SENCA had received a call from Adelaide Barlow the morning after the storm. Worried about his friend, Phil had come to assure himself that Ned was all right.

"After all, I got you into this, buddy," Phil said, as they lunched on Elsie's excellent Reuben sandwiches and chowder. "Want to keep going or call it quits? I can probably get Marty to finish the job."

"Not on your life. These past couple of months have been the best in years. I'll be fine tomorrow, but I'm stayin' 'till Friday. A few days of 'R & R' with Elsie's food is just the break I needed. You staying over?"

"Nope. Wish I could, but we're spending the weekend with Marge's folks. I gotta get back and put in two full ones if I expect to spring free Friday morning. I'd like to take a look around, but not this trip. Maybe later in August I'll come down for a few days. Bring a couple of grad students, make it a field trip."

"Great. How is Marge anyway?"

"Same, fat as a house, nagging to beat the band, you know Margie, but she loves me. What can I say? Who else would I get to put up with no money, no life, no future, no nothing?"

"That's bullshit and you know it. You and Marge have the happiest marriage of any couple I know."

"So, what about you guys?"

"Jesus, Phil, don't mention Penny and me in the same breath as you two. You wanta jinx your life?"

"She called yesterday. She'd heard about your accident and she was worried."

"How the hell did she find out about it?"

"She's still your wife, buddy. When Mrs. Barlow called, I didn't know what your condition was. I just thought she ought to know."

Phil stared at Ned, his brown eyes full of concern.

"I wish you hadn't, but forget it, it's done. Let's not talk about Penny, okay? She and I are finished. Period. She's got Martin drawing up the papers as we speak. It's all bullshit, but she can have it all. I don't give a damn about any of it except Haggardy. She hates him, but of course is hanging on to him 'cause she knows I care about him. Poor guy."

Ned closed his eyes and rubbed his temples. His head pounded. "I'm sorry, Phil. I don't mean to sound like such an asshole. It's just been a long, hard year."

"For God's sake, don't worry about me. Have you talked to the kids?"

"Just Syd. Ned and Janie are sailing somewhere with her folks, so they'll be spared the drama."

He smiled, good humor returning as the pounding in his head eased.

"So what's Mrs. Barlow like anyway? Sounded nice on the phone."

"Oh, she's nice all right. Saved my life. Though, I'm still not sure how she did it."

"What d'ya mean?"

"Well, she…" Ned paused, remembering his dream, where she had held him as they rode on some sort of sea creature. "To tell you the truth, I remember nothing after I hit my head. No memory until I woke up in her bed."

Phil whistled, "Hey, buddy that's fast work."

"Guest bed. Anyway, I don't have the slightest idea how she did it."

"Think now that you're so friendly she'll be more cordial to SENCA? Let us explore the entire island, use the dock and so forth?"

"Nope. And we aren't friendly. She helped me out because she didn't want to watch a stupid idiot drown right in front of her, but I doubt we'll be seeing each other again."

"Why not?"

"She wants to be left alone. Period. Likes her privacy and I don't think my brief stay changed her attitude about that."

"Never know. Maybe you're losing your touch? You know, out of practice after so many years of monogamy?"

Ned laughed. "As if I ever had one."

Phil stayed for most of the afternoon and even persuaded the nurse to let Ned have a beer with him. He departed before supper, after assuring Ned that the Rudders would have the canoe ready and loaded with supplies Friday morning.

Tired, his head throbbing, Ned longed for sleep. Still, he was sorry to see Phil go. Despite his enjoyment of the island's solitude, he missed companionship and conversation.

<h1 style="text-align:center">CHAPTER 22</h1>

Ned had just drifted off when the phone rang.

"Dad, it's me."

"Ned, I thought you were out in the open ocean?"

"Mom reached me when we docked in St. Kitts. I'm calling from the airport. Should I try and get up there?"

"Absolutely not! I'm fine, despite rumors to the contrary. I got a bump on the head. It was the result of my own stupidity. I don't need to be in the hospital any more than you do, but the bed's soft and they feed me well, so I'm staying 'till Friday."

"Dad, are you really okay? I mean, Mom said…"

"I'm fine, Ned. Truly. Your Mom's information is third or fourth hand. I had a mild concussion, that's all."

"Well, if you're sure?"

"I'm sure. So how's the cruising?"

"Amazing. The Richardsons have invited us to stay an extra week and the office let me off, so we're taking advantage. With Janie's condition, this might be our last chance at a vacation for a while."

"Condition? Ned, are you trying to tell me something?"

"She's pregnant. Two months along. We wanted to tell you sooner, but I didn't want to write it in a letter and you haven't called recently."

"That's terrific, son. Your mother must be over the moon."

"Well, she'd rather we were married, but she's happy, I think."

"And?"

"We're getting married the day after Thanksgiving. Baby's due in January. We want you there, Dad."

"You know I will be, Ned."

"Listen, Dad, I gotta go. You sure you're okay? Not too lonely out there all by yourself?"

"I'm fine. Thanks for calling."

"Mom's seeing Martin, you know."

"Haven't they wrapped things up yet? I've yet to see the papers."

"No, I mean, she's seeing him. They're dating."

"Oh?"

"What's that mean?"

"Means I'm happy for your mother. Martin's a nice guy. He'll be good to her."

"Dad, for Christ sakes, don't you care? Aren't you the least bit hurt or upset?"

"No Ned, I'm not. Your mom and I have been over for a long time. It's time we both get on with our lives."

"I love you, Dad. Take care."

"Love you too, son. Give my love to Janie and remember me to Betty and Steve."

"No more boat trips in the middle of hurricanes."

"It was barely a squall, for God's sake."

"Bye, Dad."

His children knew him too well. He knew they would support him in whatever he chose to do and would never judge him as Penny did. Still, he couldn't quite shake the feeling that he had disappointed them. Sometimes, it seemed as if they were the parents and he the wayward child. Did they worry about his lifestyle? Did they wish he had a regular job? Although they understood the reasons for their parents' estrangement and always took their father's side, they clearly bemoaned the break-up. He knew in their hearts, his children still hoped for reconciliation, a return to the familiar, no matter how strained and unnatural.

After a while, Ned drifted off. He slept through supper and awoke at around midnight to find a turkey sandwich and thermos of soup on the bedside table. Saying a silent thank you to Elsie, he sipped the still-hot soup and nibbled at one half of the sandwich, considering his situation. After his meal, he strolled down the hall to the window and gazed out on the harbor. A low mist shrouded the coastline, but above, the sky was clear and full of stars. He could just make out the outline of Winward Island against the horizon, but perhaps it was only clouds.

As he turned away, he determined that somehow he would go back and break down her walls. He longed to be invited once again to the peaceful hilltop cottage. He realized with a start that every fiber of his being longed to know and love his mysterious neighbor. It was crazy and he knew it, loving someone he hardly knew, but there it was.

Somehow, his thoughts, desperate as they were, brought him comfort. He drifted off to a peaceful night's sleep and woke early, his head clear. Back to normal, at last.

He considered leaving that morning, but after being assured by both the nurse and doctor that he was more than welcome to stay, he decided to remain one more day.

"Never know about relapses in cases like this," Doctor Potter pronounced, waving as he continued on his rounds, which took all of five minutes since there were only two patients, Ned and a fisherman, who had required stitches to close a nasty, but unremarkable gash in his hand. He, too, was advised to wait until Friday to go home. A bachelor, too, he enjoyed the attention and Elsie's cooking as much as Ned did and had no desire to hurry home.

CHAPTER 23

Ned finished reading a Dick Francis mystery, not one of his favorite writers, but the nurse, who was a big fan, had loaned it to him and he wanted to show his appreciation for her care and attention. When his lunch arrived, he started a silly mystery set on Martha's Vineyard, the protagonist hopelessly stupid and completely unobservant.

"There's someone coming up to see you," said Mimi, the waitress from Elsie's who had delivered the food. "Real pretty too!"

Nonplussed, he sat up. She was coming to visit him. He thought he might never see her again, and now, the object of his wild midnight fantasies was here, to see him. "Where is she?"

"Just down the hall, talking to Mrs. Beaman. I heard her asking about you. Have fun." She winked, setting the bag with sandwiches, soup and dessert on the bedside table.

The door had barely closed when it swung open again and he looked up expecting to see Adelaide Barlow. Frantically planning what he would say, his jaw dropped and he almost cried out when he saw, not Mrs. Barlow, but his wife, standing in the doorway.

"Don't look so happy to see me. You look like you've seen a ghost. Were you expecting someone else?"

"What are you doing here?"

"There, there dear husband of mine, I've come to pay my respects, like a good wife should. After all, we are still married."

"Penny, what's this about?"

"We need to talk. When Phil told me you'd been hurt, that you may be near death, I can't describe how terrified I was, so empty and lost."

"Penny, please don't."

"There you go again, pushing me away. You've been fending me off for years, Ned. I deserve to know why."

"Penny, you know as well as I do, we don't belong together. We have nothing in common, no real feelings for each other. All that's left is your angry pride at the loss of one of your possessions. That, and my indifference."

"That's just cruel! When we were first married I loved, I mean, we loved each other."

"That was a long time ago, Pen. We don't have to go through it all again, do we?"

"Martin said you'd be obstinate. He's waiting in the car. He kindly offered to drive me down. Martin has been my only source of comfort these past months, since you've turned the children against me."

"I'm glad you and Martin are together, Pen. He's a good person. He'll take care of you."

"I don't want Martin. I want you!"

She clutched the sleeves of his T-shirt. Drenched in sweat from his day spent in the un-air-conditioned room, Ned marveled at the coolness of her touch. Not a drop of perspiration glistened on her smooth, white skin. As always, her perfume overwhelmed him and he dared not take a deep breath until she moved away.

Taking hold of her hands, he cradled her shaking body in his arms. "Penny, don't cry. This isn't you."

Her light sleeveless sundress hung from her painfully thin body as she pressed against him. Her arms circled his neck and her lips moved to kiss him. He turned his head slightly and kissed her on the cheek, straightening his arms to put several inches between them.

"What do you want me to say, Pen?"

"That you love me. That this marriage should go on. That you want to make love to me. God knows, we could latch the door and they'd never know the difference."

"It wouldn't change anything, Pen. And, besides, what about Martin?"

"Martin is a friend. He's here to carry out my wishes."

"I see," he said, unsuccessful in squelching his sarcasm.

"What's that supposed to mean?"

"Let's stop this, please? I can't be there anymore, to carry out your wishes, do your bidding, any of it. I'm sorry."

Enormous brown eyes moist with tears stared back at him and Ned sighed. She was lovely. Skinny, yes, but still one of the loveliest women he'd ever seen, yet he felt nothing.

She stood, smoothing the skirt of her dress. "Well, I'm sorry, too. I'm taking everything if you don't come back and handle things. I want you to come home for a few weeks."

"Not 'till the fall. I've committed to finish the study and I intend to do just that."

"That's not good enough. You will be back in the next few weeks or that's it. I will instruct Martin to draw up the papers, giving me the house, the furniture, everything. He can do that, you know."

Weary of the fight, he said, "Fine, whatever you want, just send the papers along and I'll sign. Don't 'spose you want me to take Haggardy off your hands?"

"Fuck you, Ned," she screamed, grabbing her purse.

The door slammed. Ned listened as her footsteps clicked down the hall, then leaned back and closed his eyes. Nauseous, the pounding in his head had returned full force, blurring his vision. In their nearly twenty-five years of marriage he couldn't remember Penny swearing, not even so much as a "darn" or "damn."

CHAPTER 24

After Penny's visit, Ned paced the room, unable to read or concentrate on anything. He slept poorly that night and rose at the crack of dawn Friday morning. Eager to back to the island, he walked the halls, waiting for Doctor Potter to make his rounds and discharge him. He hitched a ride to the Pickle Shack with the night nurse going off her shift. He asked Abe and Rufus to gather his equipment and ready the boat while he ran a few last minute errands in the village.

"Hadn't expected you so early, Fielding," Abe muttered, as he and Rufus loaded the last of his provisions into the canoe.

Thanking the two men, while enduring countless warnings about storms and the Widow, Ned finally pushed off.

"Still say she's a witch. Don't let down yer guard, Fielding!"

He shook his head, waving as he putted out towards the channel. It was a clear, calm day and he reached the island well before noon and Rufus' mail delivery. He left a note, written the previous evening, in her mail chest, inviting her to dinner the following night.

He was surprised to find his garden cart waiting at the dock when he arrived. He wondered how it had gotten there. Had Rufus finally screwed up the courage to venture forth on the island without him? Or was she helping him once again? Further surprises awaited him at the camp, where he found everything tidied up and the tent repegged. The morning after the storm, he had spied the collapsed tent from the cottage's bathroom window, yet here it was, restored and looking sturdier than ever. Heartened, he hoped his neighbor had, indeed, been his unseen helper. Perhaps this gesture of friendliness boded well for his dinner invitation.

However, Ned's hopes were dashed when he went to down to collect his mail. His invitation lay at the bottom of his stack of mail, opened, with a brief message penned in a delicate hand on the back of the envelope.

"Thank you, Mr. Fielding, but I must decline. I'm afraid that, despite our brief acquaintance, nothing has changed. I value my privacy above all else and I would be very grateful if you, in turn, will honor it. A.B."

"Dammit!"

His voice echoed against the cliff walls that surrounded the cove. Self-consciously he turned, wondering if he was being watched, but the cliffs remained silent, no one visible along their stark heights.

Peevish and angry, he muttered, "The hell with you then!" and headed back to camp.

Later in the day, he made another trip to the mailboxes and left a second note in her box:

"Dear Mrs. Barlow:
With all due respect, I was in no way trying to invade your privacy. My invitation was simply a gesture of thanks for your kindness. I understand your wish for solitude. I only ask that you, in turn, respect my wish to show my gratitude to you. I will not bother you again, Ned."

Angrily thrusting the letter into her mail chest, he strode off. He fully expected her to rebuff him again, but felt better at having made the effort. Any communication was preferable to silence.

CHAPTER 25

When Ned arose Saturday morning, thick fog blanketed the island. The tent, drenched by an early morning downpour, sagged under the heavy moisture. As he pushed the flap back and stepped out, Ned's mood sank. He had hoped for a clear, cloudless day on his first day back, but rain clouds hovered like black goblins as far as he could see.

"Shit," he muttered, closing the flap, his sleeve soaked, cold droplets running down his cheeks.

He chewed on a ham and cheese sandwich left over from the previous day's lunch, then crawled back into his sleeping bag with his field journals to take stock. He would postpone the field work for another day and use today to go over all his notes and organize and plan the next few weeks.

A meticulous researcher, Ned was observant and thoughtful. His notes, hastily scribbled in the field, were cryptic and unintelligible to most readers. Therefore, he always transcribed and elaborated before too much time had passed, so that his findings could be used by others. Blessed with weeks of beautiful weather during which he refused to be inside, he had neglected the transcription for some time. Phil had asked about his notes on Wednesday. It would be good to get caught up with them.

Involved in his task, the day flew by with almost no thought about dinner or his spurned invitation. In fact, he forgot about the mail until nearly three when his growling stomach forced him to fix some lunch. There was a note from Sydney, no mention of his accident, thank goodness. At least one family member kept things in proper prospective. He also found a large envelope from the law office of Lawson & Son. Quick work, he thought as he tucked it under his arm unopened.

The reminder of Penny made him irritable. Upon his return to camp, he threw the rest of the mail on his cot, changed into his bathing suit, and headed down to the beach nearest the meadow. The sky had cleared, but the air was chilly for July. He drew his towel over his shoulders for warmth. Diving into the still-frigid water, he paddled out listlessly. When he was about a hundred feet offshore, he began stroking hard and strong, south along the coast of the island.

Swimming cleared his head and he kept on, making the turn at the southwestern point of the island. Not until he began swimming eastward, against the current, did his arms begin to tire. Ignoring them, he swam on, enjoying the view of the cliffs. This point of land, the last thing he had seen before hitting his head during the storm, was the wildest and least accessible. The underbrush, thick and unchecked, made walking slow and painful. He hadn't yet succeeded in reaching the cliffs at the point. Gulls and terns nested in its recesses. The sandy face of the rock was littered with their droppings.

Still some distance from the cove and the dock, a cramp in his left thigh forced him to stop and float for a time. After massaging the leg for several minutes, it loosened up enough for him to go on, but he had farther to go now. The current had pulled him westward. Refusing to panic, he took his time and stroked rhythmically, favoring the leg as much as possible.

Several hundred yards from the mouth of the cove, a movement behind caused him to turn back and he peered over his shoulder. Not thirty yards behind him, heading directly towards his kicking legs, a grey fin sliced silently through the water, rippling the surface just slightly as it neared him.

"Shit," he cried out, looking towards shore.

If he swam hard, he might reach shallow water, but he doubted it. Changing directions, he headed for the beach, knowing full well that he hadn't a chance.

The thing was nearly upon him when, from his side, another fin appeared, heading not for him, but for his pursuer. As Ned watched in horror, the dolphin struck what he could now see was an eight-foot tiger shark. The mammal doubled back to stride again and Ned swam for shore with every ounce of strength he could muster. Reaching shallow water at last, he stepped down and waded to his knees. Only then did he dare turn back. The battle was over and both creatures had disappeared, the sea flat and smooth once again. As he made his way along the rocky beach, he wondered if, like so many other occurrences on the island, this too had been a dream.

He reached camp, scratched and tired. His stomach reminded him of his scanty lunch. Changing, he decided on a simple meal of bread, cheese and canned soup. He had just set the soup on the stove and was laying out the bread and cheese, an unopened beer in his vest pocket, when he glanced up to see her walking towards him from across the fields.

Too shocked to move, he stood, mouth agape, as she approached. When she stopped, not five feet from him, he dropped the knife, narrowly missing his foot as it fell to the ground.

"I'm sorry. Is this the wrong night? Mr. Fielding, are you all right?"

"I didn't think you'd come. Had no idea, I mean, I'm the one who should apologize. I have nothing prepared."

She smiled. "Bread and cheese will be fine. And vegetable soup? That is, if you have enough?"

She stood, waiting for him to speak, as Ned continued to stare.

"Maybe I should go? I seem to have taken you by surprise. I guess you did not receive my note?"

"Hold on just a second."

Ned disappeared into the tent and rifled through the stack of mail. He found the thin sheet of paper sandwiched between the pages of his *Sports Illustrated*.

"I will come. Thank you. A.B."

Tearing open the tent flap, he held up the paper, aware that he must be acting like a madman.

"I missed it. The note, your note I mean. I had some discouraging mail today. I was disgusted, so I threw the whole stack aside."

She smiled, soft eyes studying him.

His wild, breathless behavior had not scared her off and Ned began to relax.

"As you can see, Mrs. Barlow, I was not expecting company, but, I'd love for you…I mean, I'd be very happy to have you stay. That is, if you don't mind eating out of a can. I understand completely if you'd rather not."

"Thank you, I'll stay. May I?" She indicated a stool near the stove.

"Please, take the chair." He pulled his canvas chair near to the stove. "Are you cold? I can start a fire, if you'd like."

"No, I'm fine, and Aran doesn't like open fires."

She gestured towards the meadow where the coyote crouched, watching her mistress.

"Yes, I expect he doesn't."

"She."

"Excuse me, she doesn't. I'd be interested in hearing about Aran. Would you like a drink?" I have beer, some excellent white wine, Bolton Vineyard's Chardonnay. Chilled, I'm happy to report. Also, seltzer and orange juice."

"A small glass of wine would be fine."

As he rambled on, Ned removed his glasses. The lenses were fogged and he cleaned them on his shirt tail.

Handsome without his glasses, she reflected, watching his befuddled performance as he rooted around, unearthing the wine and two glasses. He had beautiful green-blue eyes, like Aran's. She settled into the chair and drew her legs up. She wore blue jeans, a faded pink T-shirt and a weathered canvas jacket. Her hair was tied back in one long braid. Errant wisps framed her face, brown and rosy in the evening twilight. She let her green flip-flops fall to the ground, as she tucked up her feet and circled her arms cat-like around her calves in graceful repose.

Ned's heart skipped a beat as he returned from the refrigerator with the wine. "Here you go."

He handed her the wine, apologizing for the plastic glass, then pulled a beer from his pocket. As he twisted the cap off, foam exploded, spilling down his arms and soaking his pant leg. He grinned sheepishly.

"Must have been all that jumping up and down. Should have had wine, too, I guess."

He sat, perched precariously on the wobbly stool and an awkward silence ensued until he glanced down to spy the soup boiling over. It cascaded down inside the Coleman stove and extinguished its flame. This broke the ice and they laughed, Ned all the while fussing and fooling with the stove in a futile effort to relight it.

"Bread and cheese will be fine, truly."

"I'll give it a few minutes to recuperate, then try again. You in a big hurry?"

She shook her head. "It's nice here. Peaceful. I've often walked in this field and out along the cliffs, but I've never stopped to sit. You chose well, Mr. Fielding."

"Thanks, I think so. I fear my presence has curtailed those walks, hasn't it?"

"A little. I'm always afraid for Aran around strangers. She has no fear of people and would be an easy target."

"Tell me about Aran, if, you don't mind. How did you acquire, tame her, whatever?"

"When my husband bought the island, hunters came each fall to kill the deer. Hunting has since been banned, but the deer are gone. The hunters also shot the coyote, for sport I believe, so that by the time I came to live on Winward, most of the coyote were gone. I put a stop to the hunting, and of course your organization would not allow it either, but our efforts were too late for Aran's mother.

"When the last of the hunters left twelve years ago, they shot and left a female for dead. They didn't realize that she had just given birth, or they would have killed Aran, too. She had hidden, deep in one of the caves on the southern cliffs. I found her, starving and near death. I felt sure she would die, but I nursed her, fed her baby formula. Somehow, she survived. She's been a wonderful companion. I shall be heartbroken when she goes. She's old now, for a coyote, but still healthy."

"She certainly seems well fed."

She laughed, whistling softly. "Yes, she's quite a glutton."

Ned barely had time to blink when the creature appeared at her side, muzzle buried in her mistress' lap, begging to be petted.

"Down, Aran."

She spoke softly. The animal lay down at her feet, head resting between her paws, staring adoringly up at her mistress."

"Remarkable."

"So, Mr. Fielding?"

"Please, call me Ned."

"I do prefer Mr. Fielding, if you don't mind?" He shrugged. "How is your research coming along?"

"Fine, until my ridiculous accident. You must think me a complete fool."

"The weather changes rapidly in the channel. Anyone could have been caught as you were."

"You're being kind. But, again, I do thank you. I owe you my life."

She nodded silently, accepting his gratitude.

"I had a very curious experience this afternoon in the channel."

"Oh?"

"I swam around the southwestern point, behaving stupidly again, as it turned out, and was almost to the cove when I looked back to see a shark not thirty yards behind me."

She interrupted, suddenly anxious. "The sharks around here are relatively harmless. I expect it was simply curious."

"I never had the chance to find out. A dolphin, I believe that's what it was, came out of nowhere."

"Dolphin?" She jumped up and her wine spilled as the plastic cup clattered to the ground.

"Are you all right?"

"What happened to the dolphin?"

"He charged at the shark several times, but then I don't know. I was swimming hard for the shore and when I turned back, they were gone. Can I refill your glass?"

"Oh, I'm so sorry."

"No more apologies tonight. Okay? We're both entitled to at least three boo boos. I take it you're familiar with this creature? Am I right?" His dream of the accident, and riding on the sea creature came back to him more clearly now.

"Yes, Branwen is a friend. She carried you to shore, in the storm. She seems to have saved your life twice now, Mr. Fielding, although I doubt the shark would have bothered you. Probably a tiger shark. They don't usually go after people. They prefer smaller fish and occasionally dolphin."

"I wouldn't worry about your friend, Mrs. Barlow. She definitely had the upper hand in the encounter."

"Good." She sat back, silent for several minutes, then said, "So tell me about your study."

He launched into a long narrative about his findings thus far and his disappointment at not yet discovering signs of the burying beetles. "They're here, but I haven't run across any this season. Don't worry, you'll find them."

An attentive, careful listener, she seemed interested in his observations about the island and its inhabitants. They sat for a long while chatting and drinking wine, eventually nibbling on the bread and cheese, but forgetting the soup completely. As darkness descended, he lit the four lanterns and they sat with steaming mugs of coffee, a canopy of stars unfurling above them. While she offered little about herself, she did say, "My husband left this to me. I'm sure you've heard all about King from the villagers. They adored him."

"Yes, he did seem to be quite popular."

A pained expression came over her at the mention of her husband, so Ned changed the subject, telling her more about SENCA. After their coffee, they stretched out on the ground facing upward, stargazing. She could identify nearly as many as he, an avid, albeit amateur astronomer.

Suddenly, he turned to face her. While his head rested on his hands, she used her pet as a pillow and was therefore somewhat higher up. Feeling his gaze, she turned, staring into his eyes in the lamplight. For an instant, Ned imagined he saw his own attraction and desire reflected in her gaze.

Abruptly, she stood. "We should go. Come, Aran, up."

The dog leapt to her side.

"I'll walk you back."

Ned struggled to regroup. It had been a long time since he'd been in love. He had forgotten how overpowering the feeling was.

"Please, don't. I'll find my way. And, I suspect you might find the return trip difficult."

"I have a flashlight."

"Please, I prefer it this way. I'm fine, really. Aran is an excellent guide. We'll be home in no time."

Bowing to her wishes, he extended his hand, which she grasped in a firm handshake. "Thank you for the dinner. It's been a very long time since I've spoken more than a few words to someone. It was nice. I enjoyed your company."

Still grasping her hand, he said, "I hope you'll come again."

"I'd like that."

Gently, she extracted her hand and was gone before he could utter another sound, the two figures vanishing into the blackness of the night.

CHAPTER 26

Several weeks passed with several dinners shared, most at the camp in the meadow, one evening at the cottage. He saw little of her during the day, except from a distance, as she worked from dawn until dusk. There was not time to socialize during the daylight hours. Between her hours spent on the water, in the garden, and trips to the village to make her deliveries, she had not a minute to spare, nor did Ned. After the first dinner, she seemed to relax and Ned sensed that she looked forward to their evenings together as much as he did.

She still insisted on calling him Mr. Fielding, so he in turn, addressed her as Mrs. Barlow. She gave little clue as to her former life and looked so saddened when the subject came up that he declined to pursue it. Of one thing Ned was certain, however, this gentle woman could no more have killed another creature, not even a beast of a husband, than she could have taken the life of her beloved Aran.

As weeks passed, their friendship grew and neither could ignore their mutual attraction. Neither wanted make the first move, both of them frightened for different reasons. Although she had said nothing, there was no doubt in Ned's mind that King Barlow was the source of his widow's fear. Why else would she scream out with such terrible nightmares? Why did she shrink from his touch whenever he accidentally brushed against her? He had asked once about the nightmares, but she had shrugged and blamed them on long-held childhood fears. After a night when her screams had carried over the meadow and woken him several times, he asked again.

"I'm perfectly all right. I know, it sounds horrible. It's happened all my life. Can't stop them, I'm afraid."

She had quickly changed the subject, but Ned was certain childhood fears were not at the root of her nightmares. She was terrified of people, especially men. He feared losing her one day to the horrible, agonizing dreams, or because he said something to frighten her so that she retreated once again to her life as a recluse. So, he tread lightly and enjoyed her company, telling himself to be content with that.

Everything changed one evening in early August, an evening that followed Ned's most exciting day in the field since his arrival on Winward Island.

CHAPTER 27

Undulating waves of heat washed over the tent roof. An hour after sunrise, the air was heavy, the sun scorching. His breathing labored inside the tent, Ned stepped out, stretching. The outside air was more oppressive and he momentarily considered spending the day on the beach instead of in the field, but he would have to venture out for a little while, at least. He needed to check on the carrion for signs of disturbance.

More than halfway through the census, he was working in quadrant A-4, at the southwestern tip of the island. Fed up with other animals stealing his bait, he suspected Aran was the culprit in many of the thefts, he had developed a new system of securing the carrion. Instead of screening the dead animals, he now tied their legs to pegs, staked in the ground. Carrion beetles tended to remove an animal's fur immediately, before burying it, so that the strings tethering the food would slip off easily once denuded. He had placed several sites together in the hope that the greater concentration of carrion and the absence of the screens would carry the dead animals' scent over a wider area and attract beetles from greater distances.

Too hot to eat, he filled one thermos with coffee and another with lemonade. Then, he packed his knapsack and set out, two full canteens of water slung over his shoulder. He had not slept well. The heat and another night of screams had made for fitful sleep. Sound carried from one end of the island to the other with miraculous clarity, as the water and easterly breezes were excellent conductors.

When an easterly wind blew, her screams carried so distinctly that he felt as if they slept in the same house, just steps away from each other. He wanted to help, but knew she would resent the intrusion.

Ned reached the rock where he had set up his specimen box and set down his pack. In each area, he would set up a spot from which to work, where he stored his gear and the specimen box, covered with a tarp in case of rain. That way, he did not need to lug all the equipment back to camp each night. He rested against the rock for a few minutes, long enough to drink a cup of coffee, then set off for the nearest carrion site. He had long-since left off toting specimen jars, nets and trowels to check his traps as he no longer expected to find anything of interest. So he was totally unprepared when he reached the site.

The bait had disappeared. At first, he assumed that, once again, a larger animal had snatched the tiny mole he had left there yesterday.

"Shit," he muttered, as he prepared to pull up the pegs and set the trap again. As he leaned over, hand outstretched, he stopped mid-air when he noticed the depression directly under the spot where the dead mole had lain.

"Oh, my God," he whispered, scarcely able to breath.

Gingerly, he stepped back, then ran back to the rock for tools, jars and netting. Upon his return, he gently probed the soil and lifted and scraped away the top half-inch. He could feel the mole as he probed, its body rolled into a ball just under the surface.

After painstakingly uncovering the creature, he found it denuded, fur completely gone. He extracted his magnifying glass from his vest pocket. Sure enough, tiny eggs lay curled up in the middle of the carcass, snug and secure with a ready food supply on tap for the day when they hatched. Carefully, he covered the carcass and proceeded to two other nearby sites, where he discovered similar scenarios.

The third buried carcass was that of a mouse. He gently lifted the now-skinless animal, bagged it and carried it back to the camp, laying it on the grass while he prepared a glass-topped incubator, which he filled with dirt. He did not have high hopes for this group's survival, but he wanted to try.

After setting the carcass into the box, he covered it with a light blanket of earth and returned to A-4 to check the other sites. He found buried carrion at two other locations. Nicrophorus americanus had arrived, and arrived en masse. Leaving the other sites undisturbed, he marked them with flags and took photographs and notes as to the size and depth of the depressions and the type of carrion buried. Scattered near several of the depressions in the soil, bits of mouse and mole fur attested to the burying beetles' presence.

After two, he completed his note-taking and paused to rest. Until this moment, the heat had gone unnoticed, but now the intensity of the sun pressed down. He wanted to share his discovery with someone. Phil would go crazy, but with poor cell service, that meant a trip across the channel. Forgetting his usual reticence, he set off across the fields, then along the north-south path. When he reached the fork, he veered south along the stretch of trail leading to the cottage.

As he neared the house, he broke into a sprint, calling "hello" as he reached the yard in front of the house. When no one responded, he rushed to the door, knocked loudly, and called out.

"Hello, Mrs. Barlow! It's Ned Fielding!"

No answer. As he turned away, disappointed, he spied Aran racing towards him, her mistress right behind her. She held a trowel in one hand and had a canvas bag half-full of vegetables slung over her shoulder. In overalls, she wore a sleeveless tee shirt underneath, and a baseball cap kept her hair from her neck and shoulders.

As she neared him, worry and concern shone in her eyes and Ned thought she had never looked so lovely. He wanted to run to her and take her into his arms, holding her as he told her his news. Forget the damn beetles. He loved her!

"Mr. Fielding, are you all right?"

Mr. Fielding, he thought miserably, reality restored. "They're here! I've found them! Nicrophorus americanus!"

"Excuse me?"

"The beetles, my dear Mrs. Barlow!" With that, Ned grasped her free hand and twirled her around in a mock dance. "The carrion beetles, a whole slew of them in the southwest fields!"

She smiled, gently extracting her hand from his grasp. "Congratulations, I knew you would find them."

As they stood awkwardly smiling at each other, Ned realized he had never seen her up close in the daylight hours, except after his accident. Suddenly feeling shy, he stepped back. "Well, I'd better get back. Don't want to keep you from your work."

"I do have a great deal to do in the garden just now." She made no move to go.

"Of course." He stepped off the porch. "I didn't mean to disturb you. Please forgive me, I just had to tell someone."

"I'm glad you did. No apology necessary. I am thrilled for you and honored that you took time from your work to come and tell me. What I'm trying to say is, this calls for a celebration. Perhaps you would like to come to dinner tonight and we'll toast your good fortune? Can't stop now, in this terrible heat, when I have deliveries to make and vegetables wilting before I can pick them. It would have to be later. Would eight be okay? I have much to do and need every minute of daylight."

"Eight is perfect. Maybe I should cook the dinner since you have so much to do?"

"No, I insist."

"Can I bring anything?"

"Nothing, Mr. Fielding. This is my treat. Now, I really must get back. Come, Aran." Hoisting the burlap bag to her shoulder, she turned and was halfway down the path before Ned could say good-bye.

Unable to believe his good fortune, Ned returned to camp and spent several hours scribbling notes about the day's discoveries. At dusk, he put the notebooks away, checked the specimen box for activity, then headed for the beach for a swim.

Chapter 28

At quarter to eight, Ned headed for the cottage. Shadows played mischievously along the path in front of him. Undulating with his every step, they sometimes disappeared as trees and bushes closed in and obscured the setting sun. A half hour of daylight remained, but the air was cooling off. His swim, then splash in the stream near the camp had refreshed him, and he stepped lightly along the path, looking forward to the evening ahead, pleased and deeply satisfied with his day's accomplishments.

The census of Winward Island would have been important even without the discovery of nicrophorus americanus…an important survey of an ecologically fragile area. The island had been a valuable, precious acquisition, situated as it was directly along the Atlantic Flyway. In September, all of his energies would have to go into identifying, counting and recording his observations of the thousands of migrating birds. He had arrived too late for the spring migration and thus, had concentrated his efforts on completing the land census, knowing full well that the fall meant birds—morning, noon and night.

The screech of an osprey sounded above him. As he looked up, the hawk swooped downward and headed directly towards the cottage. He stepped into the clearing just in time to see the bird land on the railing of the porch, inches from her outstretched hand.

"It's about time."

As she chided the hawk, she fed it bits of what appeared to be fish. When she looked up and spied Ned, she drew on a heavy leather glove and held out her gloved hand to the hawk. Without hesitation, it hopped from the rail to her hand and was rewarded with another piece of fish.

"So Mr. Fielding, you finally meet Gwydyon! It is he to whom you owe your life. Without his cries, we would never have found you."

"How did you ever?"

"When you live in peace with your fellow creatures, anything is possible."

"I live in peace with my fellow creatures, Mrs. Barlow, but I've been studying ospreys along this coast for years and I've never yet known one to come for a visit."

She laughed. "Before you accuse me of witchcraft again. Yes, Mr. Fielding, don't look so surprised. I know what the villagers say, that I'm an evil enchantress. Perhaps now you agree?"

"I'm speechless, if you want to know the truth."

"Please allow me to explain. I am not a witch and I have not cast a spell over this bird. As a fledging, Gwydyon became tangled in fishing line while diving. I was nearby and was able to reach him in time. Nothing was broken, but his thrashing underwater had left him weak, unfit to fly. So, I brought him home to spend a few weeks with me. We have remained friends."

As Ned neared the porch, the bird became agitated and no amount of fish or cooing seemed to soothe him.

"He's not used to you, I'm afraid."

Rising, she circled widely to avoid coming closer to Ned. As she stepped from the porch, she lifted her hand. "Goodnight, sweet prince."

As she released him, the osprey's powerful wings flapped and he rose, circling once over their heads before he disappeared over the tree tops, headed out to sea.

"Amazing! You are truly amazing, Mrs. Barlow."

She turned, seeming not to have heard the compliment. "Come in. Everything should be ready."

Ned followed her into the house. The table was set with two places, candles already lit against the growing darkness.

"Shall we eat right away? Do you mind? It's just that the lobsters are ready."

"Absolutely, I'm starved. Can I help?"

"No, please, have a seat. There's wine on the table. Will you pour?"

After pouring the wine, he waited, feeling awkward and shy. She looked especially lovely tonight in a loose white peasant-type blouse and long blue skirt gathered at the waist with a woven sash the colors of the earth. When she returned with a basket of warm bread, she took a sip of wine, then disappeared back into the kitchen. Her hair was loosely tied back, a thin pink ribbon its only adornment.

Ned longed to take hold of her ribbons, to free her hair so it might cascade down her back as it had the day he had hid and watched her swim in the pond. Recalling that day, he blushed, his sunburned face reddening deeper just as she appeared with two bowls of cold potato soup. "Here we are."

She set down his bowl with a flourish, then noticed his expression. "Are you all right" Mr. Fielding? You look flushed. Is it too warm in here?"

"I'm fine, really. Just a sunburn."

"Are you sure?"

"Perfect. Please, don't bother about me."

Suddenly, Ned decided that he could not go on with the dinner with his guilty secret gnawing away at him. "There's something I think you ought to know. I mean, there's something I need to tell you."

As she regarded him, worry reflected in her gentle eyes. "Yes?"

"A while ago, over a month ago, before we became friends, I mean, before we were friendly. Well, I spied on you one day, Mrs. Barlow. It's not something I'm proud of, in fact, I feel pretty ashamed and stupid about the whole thing. I just thought you ought to know.

"Where did this spying, as you call it, take place? Were you peeping in my windows in the middle of the night, or watching me through a spyglass from the cliffs?" She smiled, clearly bemused by his discomfort.

"No, nothing like that. I was…oh, shit, excuse me. I know I'm gonna regret this, but I was watching you from the bushes at the edge of your pond while you and Aran were swimming."

"I see."

"I'd understand completely if you'd rather I left now."

"Were we in the water the entire time you watched?"

"No, I'm afraid I remained long enough to see you emerge."

"Oh, I see. Well, then, we're even." She smiled and picked up her spoon.

"Excuse me?"

"We've both had the opportunity to study each other, clothed and unclothed. Or, are you forgetting, Mr. Fielding, that you found yourself in dry clothes when you woke after your accident?"

Speechless, he stared at her. Her eyes sparkled with mirth as candlelight danced in their depths.

"It's all right, Mr. Fielding. I forgive you. Please, let's eat the soup or the lobsters will be overcooked and soggy!"

Laughing, Ned lifted his spoon to his lips. The soup was delicious. Delicately seasoned, its creamy coolness a perfect antidote to the day's heat. He gave himself over to enjoying it, too timid to ask for seconds, too flabbergasted to speak anyway.

Midway through the lobsters, conversation resumed, relaxed and comfortable. The incident at the pond was apparently forgotten. Nearly two and a half pounds each, the lobsters were sweet and succulent. This course was followed by bread and a salad of exotic greens, some bitter, some buttery, some bland and cool, most of which Ned had never seen before. Mixed with the greens were young nasturtium blossoms, freshly cut sorrel, parsley and scallions and thin slivers of firm, summer tomatoes.

"I haven't the faintest idea what's in it, but this salad is wonderful."

"Thank you. Someday, I'll take you on a tour of the garden and point out the various ingredients. I love to experiment, try new varieties of lettuce and greens. They grow very well on the island. The soil and the air seem to give them an unusual quality, or so I've been told. Most are sold to a restaurant in Boston. The owner meets me in the village every Tuesday and Friday morning. He's very particular. The rest, I sneak into my regular customers' baskets, the adventuresome ones, at least. They've never complained."

"And well they shouldn't. Do you ever need help with all of this? I don't see how one person can garden, fish, deliver, do all that you do and still be standing."

"I manage, Mr. Fielding and to answer your question, no, I work at a pace I know I can manage. If I'm tired, I rest, and I have some reserves, some money to fall back on, if I become ill or if I'm injured or hurt."

"From your husband?"

Instantly, Ned regretted his words as the color drained from her face and what appeared to be anger flashed in her eyes.

"I'm sorry. That's none of my business."

"No, the money is my own. What I have put away over the years."

Her voice had gone cold and flat. Try as he might to engage her in other topics, a pall seemed to have been cast over the meal after the mention of King Barlow. Finally, as they finished dessert, a light, creamy flan surrounded by fresh raspberries, she seemed to relax and the gloom lifted, light once again reflected in her gaze.

Ned had just finished telling her how much the day's discovery meant to him. She rose to clear the plates and congratulated him yet again. Ned wondered as he watched her, what he always wondered. What kind of marriage would leave such scars after so many years? What kind of marriage had it been that she still cried out in terror twelve years after her husband's death?"

After clearing the dessert things she returned with two fluted glasses, her good mood clearly restored. "Here, why don't you take these to the porch and I'll join you in a moment." When he hesitated, she said, "Go ahead now. I'll be right out. Aran will keep you company."

Led by the coyote, Ned went to sit on the porch. A slight breeze blew, the air still warm, but refreshing. He settled down, relaxed and satisfied after the wonderful meal. Presently she appeared, something hidden behind her back. She stood directly in front of him, and with a smile and a "tah dah," she produced a chilled bottle of champagne, very expensive champagne.

Speechless, Ned stared up at her.

"To celebrate your discovery. Would you kindly do the honors?"

Recovering, he rose to take the bottle. He wanted to ask where she had gotten the wine, but stopped himself, unwilling to risk spoiling the mood again. After popping the cork, he filled both their glasses. They clinked their glasses softly, then sipped their wine, staring into one another's eyes. For a very long time, they sat thus, in companionable silence, aware only of each other, as they sipped their wine on the steps of the porch.

CHAPTER 29

The delicate flutes clinked together after Ned filled their glasses for the third time.

"Thank you for this…for the wine, the dinner, everything. It's been a long while since anyone celebrated an achievement of mine. You've made me feel very special, Mrs. Barlow. I know, that sounds corny, but it's been a long while since anyone made me feel this way."

"I'm glad." She set down her glass and reached out to stroke the coyote's back.

Afraid he might once again spoil the mood with his rambling, he remained silent.

"Did you have an important job, back home?"

"Not really. I used to teach biology at the college level and now I work for SENCA when they have projects like this. Let's talk about you. Much more interesting. Tell me about your childhood, your growing up."

"My parents died when I was quite young. I was raised by my mother's sister, Mildred and her husband, Wes McCully. They lived in Derryville. Do you know it?"

Ned shook his head.

"It's very much like Tripp's Landing. Small town. Everyone knows everyone."

"And everybody's business, too. How'd you meet your husband?"

"He owned a business in Derryville. A seafood processing plant. He was as popular and well-respected there as he was in Tripp's Landing."

"Was he worthy of respect?"

As he spoke, Ned poured more champagne into their glasses, watching her expression. She turned away, then rose to step down from the porch, sloshing wine on his pants as she passed by.

"I'm so sorry."

"Don't be silly, it's nothing. I'm the one who should be sorry. I didn't mean to upset you."

"I'd rather not talk about my husband, if you don't mind, Mr. Fielding. He was…it's just complicated."

"Not another word. Subject closed."

They began walking down the garden path, Aran trailing along beside her. Ned carried the wine bottle and they walked to the edge of the pond where they sat on the flat, table rock at the water's edge. She told him about the garden and the early years of hard work, clearing the land and removing rocks and boulders.

"Sometimes I'd spend a whole week on one boulder. I got very good with the lever and pick ax."

He told her about his work, the SENCA research, and his time at the college. He had already told her a bit about his children, but said nothing about Penny.

He knew this omission on his part had led her to believe that he was no longer married, but it had, until this point, seemed unimportant. Suddenly, as they sat talking, brushing against one another as they conversed, his omission seemed dishonest.

The touching had been accidental at first, as one or the other of them had shifted position or moved to pour more wine, but as the bottle became lighter and their talk became more animated, they relaxed, and the touches became intentional, gentler and more intimate. In the midst of a tale about Abe Rudder and his wild rumors and superstitions, she reached over and touched his arm.

"Don't blame Abe too much. I'm afraid I've rather encouraged him. He never liked me, even when my husband was alive. He worked for the Barlows for years. He had adored the first Mrs. Barlow. Never quite got over his employer taking a second wife, especially one so much younger. When I first came to live at Windtop, the Rudders lived on the grounds of the estate, returning to their home in the village on weekends. Then Abe and my husband had words and the Rudders moved away. Even so, they remained close."

"What was their quarrel?"

"I have no idea. With King, almost anything could set him off."

"So he had a temper?"

"Terrible." She shuddered and Ned feared he might lose her again.

"Shall we star gaze for a while?" He reached out, took her hand, and led her to the grassy clearing nearby.

"Let's not dwell on the past," he whispered, taking her gently in his arms as they sat down. "Too many ghosts."

She nodded, her hand stroking his arm.

"So beautiful," he said, voice husky as his hand cupped her chin and drew her to him, their lips meeting in a soft kiss.

She trembled and Ned could feel her terror. "Is this okay?"

"Yes," she murmured, her arms circling his neck. "Please don't stop."

He kissed her again, more deeply, his tongue parting her lips.

"I love you," he whispered, moving down to kiss her neck, his hands caressing her firm, round breasts.

She wore no bra, her nipples hard and erect under the thin peasant blouse. He unbuttoned her blouse and cupped her breasts, then bent to kiss the soft, smooth skin. His tongue traced a circle around each perfect nipple and she moaned, crying out in pleasure as she pressed against him. Before he knew it, she had slipped out of her skirt, and lay beside him, naked except for her panties. Under his touch, her body writhed, his caress answered with a sigh from deep within her.

Somehow, Ned struggled out of his clothes and their bodies came together, her warmth driving his passion to the limit. He willed himself to go slowly. Her passion matched his, but she still trembled and he had no wish to hurt her. Gently, he kissed her neck and breasts, then moved down to part her legs. He stroked her thighs as his lips and then his tongue found her soft folds and she cried out again. When he entered her, their bodies moved in perfect unison, the sensual, depth of their lovemaking a feeling that Ned had never experienced. Lost, he gave himself over completely, crying out in love and ecstasy.

Afterwards, they rested on the grass, still holding one another tightly, unwilling to let go.

"I meant what I said, my darling. I love you, Adelaide Barlow. I've loved you since the day I watched you swimming from my cowardly hiding place in the bushes, loved you as I've never loved a woman before."

"Ned," she murmured, nestling against him, tears bathing his shoulders.

"Hey, what's that? No more Mr. Fielding?"

She laughed and held him tighter, sobbing now.

"Sh, my darling. It's all right. Whatever happens, it's all right. You're safe with me. No one will ever hurt you again."

He held her for a long while, before standing to pull her up beside him.

"What do you say to a swim? Any creatures likely to bother us in your pond? Leeches, snapping turtles, killer toads?"

Laughing, she took his hand. "Come on."

They ran into the water together. Aran, who had wandered off during their lovemaking, jumped in to join them and the three paddled in unison to the far end of the pond. There, the coyote left them, to hunt in the brush above the waterfall.

As they stood in the shallow water, the water cascading down, splashing against their backs, she draped her arms round his neck and planted a kiss on Ned's shoulder. "Usually, she never leaves my side. She must know I'm safe with you. Am I, safe with you? Will you protect me?"

"I'll do more than protect you, my beautiful Addie. It's okay if I call you Addie, isn't it?"

She nodded shyly and Ned pulled her close, spreading her legs apart, and drawing them around his waist. This time, as he entered her, their lovemaking was slower, gentler. They stood under the waterfall, bringing each other to glorious climax once again, and this time Ned's tears of joy joined hers.

Later, when they reached the water's edge, she seemed spent, almost unable to walk. Ned gathered their clothes and flung them over his shoulder then lifted her into his arms and carried her back to the cottage. Aran padded soundlessly along behind. It felt to Ned as if he was carrying one of his children to bed, rather than his lover. So young and so vulnerable she was. Despite her passion and strong feelings, he was acutely aware of her sexual inexperience. Again, he wondered about King Barlow and what he had inflicted on such a gentle creature.

By the time they reached her bedroom, she was half asleep. He lay her down gently, covered her with a quilt, and kissed her goodnight, rising to go.

She stirred and reached for him. "Please don't leave me. Stay?"

Ned slipped beneath the sheets and their bodies came together again, this time for warmth and comfort until they slept, the dreamless sleep of lovers sated and spent.

CHAPTER 30

"Addie, that was incredible." Ned sighed, relishing the last bite of his blueberry scone. "Would you rather I call you, Adelaide?"

"Addie, please. My father used to call me Addie. I don't remember him well, but I do remember that."

He smiled and reached out to take her hand. Addie sat beside him on the bench as sunlight danced along the whitewashed walls of the kitchen. "This is a rarity for me. It's not often that I take time to savor breakfast."

"Nor I. I'd be out of business if I slept this late! And the woodchucks would have long since taken over the garden."

"I meant, I haven't much experience with this. No, that's not what I wanted to say either. I've been married for such a long time and there have never been any times like this."

She gave him a sweet, sad smile…her sweet, sad smile. He noticed that her slender fingers gripped the worn pine table. "You don't have to explain, really you don't."

"Yes, I do. What I want to say is, I love you Addie Barlow. I'm not sure I've ever really been in love before. Ever. I'm tongue tied and scared you'll wake up from this dream we're in and kick me out. I want to take you in my arms and hold on for dear life. None of what I feel is rational, sensible, or in line with anything that's ever happened in my life before. It's a little unnerving at my age to suddenly feel like an adolescent."

She stood. "I understand. Now, I've got to go. Please stay and rest, but I've got deliveries."

"Addie, what's wrong?"

"Nothing. Please, I must go." Her eyes had misted over and tears threatened to spill.

"Will I see you later?"

"As you wish," she answered with bowed head, refusing to meet his eyes.

Ned grabbed hold of her arm. "No, it's not as I wish. I want to know what you wish. Please tell me what I've said to upset you."

Her body went limp, then she began to tremble. "Let me go, please."

"God, I'm sorry, Addie. I didn't mean to. Can I stop by and see you later on?"

She nodded and slipped out the back door without another word, Aran at her heels.

He stood, stepping to the doorway. "Supper at my place?"

She paused with her back to him, shoulders limp. "What time?"

"Seven? Or six, or five or eight. Anytime you say."

"I'll be there at seven. Bye." Her voice sounded a little lighter, thank goodness.

After washing the dishes, Ned gathered his things, and headed back to camp. It was nearly eleven when he had collected his gear and headed out for the field. He planned to work until two, then head across the channel to get provisions for dinner. Addie's was not the only work day that would be less than productive. 'Who cares?' he thought, hoisting his pack to his back. Wait until Phil hears about the beetles.

CHAPTER 31

Addie arrived just before sunset. Barefoot, she wore jeans and a blue cotton sweater. Her beautiful eyes, dark pools in the twilight, stared right through him, her expression unreadable. The round, firm contours of her breasts were barely concealed beneath the thin, gauzy knit of the sweater and he felt his manhood stir, fully aroused. Completely unaware of her effect on him, she smiled.

Ned smiled back and reached out his hand. Relieved to see her, he had worried all day that she might not come. "You're a welcome sight."

She ignored his outstretched hand and took a seat on the stool to his right. Bringing up his marriage had clearly upset her. Not ready to discuss Penny, he asked, "Where's Aran?"

"Hunting, I expect. Can I help?"

"Nope. Everything's about ready. Just have to boil the linguine. The pesto's not as good as yours, but, it's edible, I think."

"I'm sure it will be delicious."

"Would you like to eat now or wait awhile?"

"Now, please, if you don't mind. I'm starving."

Ned wasn't sure whether to laugh or cry at her polite and formal tone, but he turned away to busy himself with the dinner preparation. He had fresh tomatoes and cucumbers sliced and drizzled with olive oil and a loaf of crusty French bread, courtesy of Ivy, to serve with the pesto. Fresh peaches topped with very soft ice cream would be their dessert.

After plunging the pasta into the pot of boiling water, he poured them each a glass of wine and came to sit beside her. "Want a chair?"

"No, I'm fine."

"Addie." Ned removed his glasses and rubbed his eyes. A nervous habit, he invariably fiddled with his glasses when upset, often cleaning them repeatedly during times of stress. It had always been a source of annoyance to Penny, who would scream in the middle of a tirade, "put your glasses on, so I can look you in the eye!" Addie found the gesture endearing and her gaze softened.

"I want to explain to you about Penny, my wife."

Her hand shot up and she stood. "Please don't. You don't owe me an explanation. It's none of my business."

"Of course it's your business. I love you. Please sit down and hear me out. It would mean a lot to me." He held her hand and his eyes pleaded.

Addie sat back on the stool, her eyes brimming with tears.

"I have to be honest. This is one of my least favorite subjects—my marriage and what's wrong with it. I try to never talk about it, if I can avoid it. Penny has not been a part of my life for a very long time. In fact, I often forget about her altogether. Sounds awful, huh?"

"But you have children."

"Grown children, adults now. We were friendly enough in the early years. Both our kids were born before we moved back to Greenleaf, the town where we grew up, where my in-laws lived. I cared for Penny in those early years. It wasn't the same as the feeling I have for you, but there was affection, warmth and passion." He looked up to see if his words were upsetting her, but Addie listened, eyes dry, demeanor calm. She no longer appeared sad or angry, just curious.

"We married very young. Penny was four months pregnant with Ned at the time. It was kind of fun those first years…on our own, struggling to make ends meet while I was in graduate school. Then, we moved back to Greenleaf, and Penny changed. I changed too, I guess.

"Her life in Greenleaf has never included me. My choice, not hers. Can't blame Penny for the lack of trying. She tried every trick in the book to get me involved in the country club, the parties, and the social functions that went on year-round. She thrived on all of it—she's very civic-minded. I hated every blessed second of it.

"I was a real jerk. Full of contempt and ridicule for things that were really important to Pen. Penny's a terrific mother, always has been, and she's a good person. She deserved much better than me.

"So, there you have it. Sad tale, huh? It's been over six years since we've slept together, in the same bed, I mean, never mind sex. Until recently, we lived under the same roof, but we might as well have lived a hundred miles apart. We rarely spoke, never went out together, or sat at the table for a meal, unless the kids were home.

"The divorce should be final soon. Did I tell you I'm gonna be a grandfather early next year?"

"Yes, you did." She smiled and her shoulders relaxed. "Where will you live, after the divorce? Will you return to your home, or will your wife?"

"Ex-wife." He let a trace of bitterness creep into his voice. "No, I won't be going back to the house, except to pick up my things. Penny's taking everything—house, the furniture, even good old Haggardy."

"Haggardy?"

"My dog. I'm crazy about him. Penny hates him, but she'll hang onto him out of spite."

"Maybe she'll change her mind?"

He shrugged and took hold of her hands. "Hey, let's talk about something else. Okay?"

She nodded, subject closed. Despite Ned's boiling the pasta for nearly twenty minutes, dinner turned out remarkably well. Lost in conversation, neither one of them noticed or cared about the soggy, overcooked linguini. She was interested in his latest finds and made several suggestions.

Addie also told him about an encounter with Rufus Rudder in the village. "He actually said hello to me."

"Rufus isn't so bad when you get him away from his old man. He's comin' around. In fact, he's sneaked onto the island a couple of times for a beer with me."

"Uh, oh. You better hope Abe doesn't find out!"

They laughed, rising to clear the supper dishes by the light of a full moon.

After cleaning up, they strolled towards the cliffs, holding hands. "This is where I first saw you," he whispered, turning to take her into his arms.

She returned his embrace, kissing his neck, her lips softly brushing against his skin. "Mmm."

"Stay with me, Addie. It's not as comfortable as your bed, but I want you to stay. I want to sleep out under the stars with you in my arms."

In answer, she looked up and kissed him, lightly at first, then with more urgency. Slipping his glasses off, Ned returned her kisses, his tongue parting her lips to delve deeply. His voice gruff with emotion, he whispered, "My dear, sweet, Addie."

He lifted her, wrapping her legs around him as he carried her back towards his camp.

They made it as far as the grass growing at the edge of the cliff before he set her down, slipped her sweater over her head, and began fumbling with the zipper of her jeans.

"Here, let me."

Her voice was silky soft, caressing his ear as she slipped out of the jeans. She wore no undergarments, her soft, dark mound clearly visible against the white of her skin. The moonlight shining on her nakedness took Ned's breath away as it had that day when he'd watched her from the bushes. He moaned, an involuntary sound from deep within, while at the same time feeling her hands under his shirt, caressing, drawing him closer with each breath.

"What about you?" she murmured. "You're still fully clothed. We'll have to do something about that."

As she slipped his T-shirt over his head, his hiking shorts and boxers fell together. Ned kicked them aside with a flourish and lifted her, spreading her legs, his desire almost overpowering him.

"No," he cried, drawing breaths in great gulps to calm himself. "This isn't fair. You're not ready."

"Please," she moaned as her hand guided him into her soft moist recesses. Ned entered her and thrust gently, deeper and deeper, lost in ecstasy and love. As his legs wobbled, she brought hers downward, holding him deep inside of herself, as they lowered themselves to the grass. Astride him now, she matched him thrust for thrust, moaning and crying out as her climax washed over her.

Ned held back as long as he could, enjoying her pleasure, suckling her breasts, kissing her lips and her long slender neck. He felt her every movement acutely, the pain of restraint almost unbearable. Finally, she reached down to him. Her kisses drove him wild and release came in undulating waves of pleasure, the ground afire beneath his trembling body.

"Addie, my darling, darling Addie," he murmured, bringing her down to rest on his chest. His arms encircled her, holding tight.

"I love you, Ned Fielding."

Tears stung his eyes. Never had any words meant so much.

They lay on the grass for a long while before rising to walk arm in arm back to camp.

Ned brought out the two old comforters he used as a mattress and lay them on the grass. Over these, he spread his sleeping bag splayed open, fully unzipped. Lying down beside her, he pulled a thin cotton blanket over them. The air was warm, but a breeze blew across the meadow and the blanket felt good against his skin. Her nearness aroused him, but he held back, demanding no more from her. Spent and tired, her body trembled. She needed to sleep.

The scream seemed to come from inside of him as it pierced the stillness of the moonlit night. Ned reached for Addie, startled to discover she was no longer at his side. Groping about for his glasses, he muttered, "Shit" and abandoned his search. He heard movement not far from him, accompanied by low, pitiful moans.

Then she screamed again. "No, no! King. Please. No!!"

Spying her writhing form curled up on the grass several feet from the blankets, he crawled to her and took her trembling body into his arms. "It's all right, Addie, Sh."

"No!" She screamed and he braced himself, expecting her to flail out at him. Instead, as his arms held her tighter, she went limp, all the life suddenly drained out of her.

"Addie?" She was still asleep, weeping silently, her tears cold on his chest. "My dear, sweet Addie," he murmured, picking her up. "What did that monster do to you?"

He lifted her and carried her back to the sleeping bag where he lay down with her against him. Afraid to sleep, lest she pull away lost in another night terror, he lay awake, the stars blinking and watchful in the clear sky above him. When the first rays of sun lit up the eastern horizon he dozed off, assured she was safe in the light of day.

CHAPTER 32

When he woke, Ned found her up and fully dressed, boiling water for tea. He watched her for several minutes before speaking. She looked serene and peaceful. It was difficult to reconcile the calm presence before him with the wild, frightened creature, who had thrashed in his arms just a few hours earlier.

"Good morning."

"You're up." She smiled and came to him, shyly kissing his chest, then his lips. Returning her embrace, he felt his ardor rise. He longed to strip off her clothes and draw her close, losing himself again in lovemaking so powerful it frightened him, but he held back, recalling the screams.

She saw his expression and pulled back. "Took me a good while to locate my clothes. I found yours. Do you want them, or shall I?" She moved as if to lie down beside him.

"Addie, please tell me about it, about your marriage. I don't want to cause you pain. God knows, I would never intentionally hurt you, but your dreams… you're so frightened."

"Did I have a nightmare? I'm sorry." She turned away, but not before Ned glimpsed the pain mirrored in the depths of her dark eyes.

"Addie, for God's sake. What did he do to you?"

"I can't." She stood. "I've got to go. There's so much work to do and we slept so late."

Forgetting the two mugs of coffee on the table, she grabbed her sweater and headed for the path.

"Addie, please don't go like this."

Ned chased after her, feeling awkward and foolish as he loped through the open fields, still naked.

Finally, she stopped and turned back, waiting for him to draw near. For an instant, a smile flickered in her eyes, but her words kept him at bay. "Please, Ned, leave me alone. I need to be by myself."

"I want to help you, Addie. I love you. Whatever that bastard did to you, it's over! He can't hurt you anymore."

"Please, stop. I beg you, I can't." Her face was streaked with tears, eyes, wild and terrified, beseeched him.

"Will I see you tonight?"

"I'll find you." With that, she disappeared into the thicket that bordered the meadow.

CHAPTER 33

Late that night, long after he'd eaten, she appeared out of the darkness, Aran at her side. Relief washed over Ned as he reached out for her. Before she could speak, he blurted out, "Addie, I'm sorry. I won't ask you again. If you don't want to tell me, I'll back off. I can't spend another day like today, wondering if I'll ever see you again. Please forgive me."

"There's nothing to forgive. It's time I explained, but might I have a glass of wine?"

"Of course, my darling. Have you eaten? Would you like something?"

She shook her head, "Just the wine will be fine."

Fumbling around with relief and happiness, he managed to produce two cups and sloshed chardonnay over their rims. She had already taken the chair, forestalling the usual fussing that ensued until she agreed to take it. He sat on the stool beside her. He attempted to take her hand, but she withdrew slightly, seeming to need the distance to collect herself.

"When I think back on it, King courted my aunt and uncle, not me. I think he knew that, with their approval, I'd go along quietly. He was right. I did. King was awfully kind to us all. I'm afraid I mistook kindness for love.

"To a naïve eighteen-year-old, King Barlow promised adventure and excitement. He was much older than me. Fifty-five at the time of our marriage. A trifle overweight, he was still good-looking, some would say handsome."

She went on to tell him about her wedding night, the pain, and the savagery of his assault. Her voice was flat, expressionless as she proceeded through her narrative. It was as if he were listening to a stranger reciting horrible events in a fractured, distant monotone, as if she had stepped out of herself, and was an observer to the incidents she described.

"My poor darling. Why didn't you leave him?"

"Stupid as it seems, I didn't know any better. My aunt had told me nothing about sex beyond the fact that it might hurt the first time."

"God, what a nightmare."

"Yes, it was, but you mustn't blame my aunt. Like everyone else, she adored King. That he would treat me cruelly would never have crossed her mind. She considered our marriage a fortunate, happy occurrence."

"Did you have anyone to talk to? Anyone who could help?"

"Not at first, but later. I didn't stay naïve and innocent for long. As time passed, the beatings became more frequent." She paused, her voice quavering. "My husband drank too much. His doctor warned him repeatedly, but King paid no attention. When he drank, which was every night, he became abusive.

"Before we were married, I had been honest with him. I'd told him that, while I was fond of him, I didn't love him. He assured me that this made no difference, that he would win my love once we were married. Later, he used my honesty to torment me and to justify the abuse.

"I could see it in his eyes, when he was preparing to come after me. He'd glare, then dare me to speak. I would run upstairs and lock my door, but it was no use. He had keys or he'd break down the door. I can't tell you how may times the man had to come to repair that door.

"He would chase me, screaming out, 'do you love me yet, my darling Adelaide?' I pleaded with him, but that only made things worse. Sally knew, Sally Mendoza, our housekeeper. The first few times, she tried to intervene, but I believe he threatened her. I don't know exactly what he said or did. Sally was very fond of the first Mrs. Barlow and did not really approve of me. Perhaps she thought it was my fault.

"Eventually, others found out. During the second summer of our marriage, he broke my nose. He took me to Boston for treatment. The doctors recognized the signs of abuse…the bruises and the burns."

Ned shuddered. "Burns?"

"I've been waiting for you to notice and ask about them. Perhaps, passion has blinded you?" She smiled, pain reflected in her eyes, the lantern's light, revealing a well of sorrow.

She rose, unbuttoned her jeans, slipped them down to her knees, and spread her legs slightly. How he had missed them? Ned stared at the raised red welts along the tops of her inner thighs. Round, angry marks lined the opening between her legs, five on each side.

"King smoked cigars," she said quietly, pulling on her jeans, and sitting down.

"Oh, my God, Addie." Ned stood and reached for her.

"No, please, Ned. Now that I've started, I want to finish."

Ned sat, tears blinding him. He did not want to hear another word.

"The doctors saw the burns. King called them his 'brand.' He said I belonged to him and once I had his mark, no one would dare to touch me.

"Doctor Slocum recommended that I seek residential treatment. He offered to help me. I thanked him and promised to think about it, but I came home with King after all. By that time, I was no longer sane, had no idea what I was doing or how to help myself.

"Doctor Slocum also talked to King. After that, King told me that if I ever spoke to anyone about what happened in our bedroom, he'd kill me and my aunt, too. Uncle Wes had already passed away by that time and my aunt was not well.

"Strange as it might seem, there were times when King could be tender, even solicitous of my feelings. It never lasted long. The night he burned me…" She paused, face suffused with pain.

"Addie, don't. It's upsetting you too much. Don't tell me any more."

Ignoring him, she went on. "We'd been to a wedding, a village girl, Susie MacIntyre. It was a lovely June day and they, the bride and groom, were so happy. The MacIntyres were not well-off; I believe King paid for all or a good portion of the reception. Greg MacIntyre did odd jobs at Windtop from time to time and King liked him. There was a tent, beautiful flowers, delicious food—courtesy of Elsie, and music for dancing.

"King enjoyed showing me off in public and had insisted that I buy a new dress for the occasion. He let me choose it. It was a simple dress with a wide skirt, a blue floral print. I liked it very much. He made a great show of whirling me around the dance floor, but then he tired and sent me off. He wanted to sit with his cronies, drinking and talking.

"I didn't care. I loved watching the dancers. And, I've never minded being alone. I hadn't been standing long when a man approached me. Jim Talbot, a lawyer from Derryville. I'd seen him in the village, but didn't know him well. Later on, I got to know Jim a little better, but at that time, he was a stranger.

"Jim is a shy, self-effacing man and I suspect he approached me because he sensed a kindred spirit. Anyway, we talked for a while. He asked me to dance, but I declined, fearful of King's jealousy. I never saw Jim again until after King's death, but I remembered his kindness to me. He was my lawyer at the inquest.

"By the time we left the party, King was very drunk. Abe Rudder drove us home. King was quiet on the drive home, perhaps he even slept, I don't remember. I prayed as we came up the drive at Windtop that he would pass out and sleep it off.

"I had just slipped into bed when he entered the room. He wore a loose dressing gown, opened in the front and I could see that he was naked beneath it. We'd been married for almost four years at the time of the wedding. By then I knew what he was capable of and wanted no part of his drunken attentions. He saw the fear in my eyes and came to sit beside me on the bed. "Sh, my darling," he crooned, his voice soothing.

"I pulled back and begged him to leave me alone. He continued speaking in soothing tones. I knew it was useless to struggle. It would only make him angrier. So, I lay still and waited. He removed my nightgown, tenderly kissing me, stroking my body, whispering. He kissed me between my legs."

Ned seethed with anger, his stomach churning. "Addie, you don't have to tell me this."

"Despite his cruelty, he knew how to arouse me, and try as I might, I succumbed to his kisses, to his touch. The shame of it haunts me still."

"Oh, Addie."

"He often forced me to take him inside my mouth, but not this night. He said over and over it was to be my night, my pleasure. And I believed him. As he kissed me, he spread my legs apart and ran his fingers up and down them, squeezing and caressing. Before I knew what was happening, he had slipped two of his ties, already knotted, around my ankles and tied them to the bedposts."

Ned groaned.

"My hands were still free and I rose up and struggled to free myself. He had tied me up once before, entered me and raped me repeatedly, then left me tied to the bed for two days."

She shook violently now and Ned suddenly began to fear for her sanity.

"He slapped me hard, stunning me just for an instant. That gave him the time he needed. He had two more ties knotted and ready and he slipped them over my wrists and secured my arms to the bedposts. The silk cut into my skin and I begged him to loosen the scarves, to set me free. He just laughed, and began his taunts, 'So, you have a lover, do you? The King not good enough for you?'

"I asked him what was he talking about, but he just continued to circle the bed, ranting and raving about my lover. He left the room for several minutes and I prayed he'd gone to bed. I struggled unsuccessfully to free myself, but the knots held fast.

"When he returned, he carried a bottle of Scotch and was smoking a cigar. He continued to circle me, carrying on about my lover. I finally realized that he was talking about Jim Talbot. He had seen us talking at the wedding.

"Suddenly disgusted, I told him he was being ridiculous, that I barely knew Jim Talbot and that his jealousy was totally without foundation. I told him he was crazy and I screamed at him to let me go, screamed for Sally to come and help me. She was in the house that night, she had to have heard.

"My screams incensed him and he came at me, the bottle brandished above his head. I closed my eyes against the blow, but nothing happened. When I opened my eyes, he stood looking down at me, grinning. 'That's what you want, don't you? You want me to end it all for you, don't you? Well, it will never be that easy, my dear.'

"As he spoke, he set down the bottle. For several minutes, he eyed his cigar, which he had placed on the edge of the night table, its thick ashes falling on the white carpet below. Then, he removed his dressing gown and climbed on top of me.

Eyes dry, Addie shook violently as she held her stomach. For a moment, Ned thought she might vomit.

"Mercifully, it didn't hurt, when he entered me. His previous attentions had left me moist. When he finished, he flopped off and I thought he might actually be asleep. Unfortunately, he was not and he soon stood, retrieved his gown from the floor, as well as his bottle and cigar from the nightstand.

"He whispered, 'My dear, you belong to me.' His eyes were full of hate and I shrank from his touch. I pleaded with him to free me, to let us both go to bed, but he only laughed. 'No, my dear Adelaide, I'm not through with you yet.'

Then he began talking about branding me, putting his mark upon me. He brought the cigar close to my face and I screamed. Again he laughed, 'Don't worry, my dear. I wouldn't dream of marring that lovely face. Just lie still, it will all be over soon.'

"He sat full upon my right leg and wrenched the left leg apart. He held the cigar and—"She broke into uncontrollable sobs, and once again Ned tried to take her into his arms.

"No, let me finish. Sally Mendoza had to have heard my screams, but she did nothing. I screamed and screamed until I passed out from the pain. When I woke the next morning, I was untied and my wounds had been dressed and bandaged. I never knew who dressed my wounds, but I made my first attempt to leave King that day. I only got as far as the Derryville bus depot before he found me and brought me back. I was sick, feverish and in no condition to fight him.

"Later, I tried again to get away. An emergency room nurse in Providence was assisting me. I'd been admitted with cracked ribs. She was very kind. She offered to let me stay with her for a few weeks until I got my bearings. I took down her address and kept it. I even tried to call her several months later, but she had moved by then. I was devastated, but shortly after, King died and I was released."

"But—"

"That's all. Now, you see what kind of person you've fallen in love with. A spineless woman who couldn't take care of herself."

Sobs wracked her body.

"Addie, for God's sake. What you've been through, no one should live through. I'm so sorry my darling, so sorry for the unspeakable suffering you endured. I'm here and always will be. Thank God he can't hurt you anymore."

For what seemed like hours, Ned held her. As the night grew cold, he carried her into the tent and zipped her into his sleeping bag. After extinguishing the lanterns, he came in, zipping himself in beside her.

They slept soundly. No nightmares disturbed her sleep. The rain on the tent woke them at daybreak, its gentle rhythm soothing. Soon after they rose, the sky cleared and a faint rainbow appeared.

"Let's agree to start over," he whispered, kissing her nose and they turned to gaze at the soft arc of colors. "Let's put the past, both of our pasts, behind us and never look back. What do you say, my darling?"

Addie leaned against him, silent and still. Finally, she squeezed his hand and rested her head against his shoulder.

CHAPTER 34

"Addie, for the last time…Phil's a great guy. You'll love him."

"Please don't push me on this, Ned. I'd just as soon keep to myself while they're here. It's only a few days."

"Whatever you say," he snapped, instantly regretting his impatient tone.

"I'm sorry," he said gently. "I know it's hard, but if you change your mind, I know you'd like Phil."

He winked at her, gratified to glimpse a hint of a smile in the dark, sad eyes. It had been two weeks since she'd told him about King Barlow's brutalities. They'd not spoken of it again, but a pall seemed to have settled over their relationship.

The telling of her story left Addie feverish and drained. Listlessly, she harvested the vegetables, fruits and herbs but could not seem to find the strength for fishing. Ned pitched in and pulled the lobster pots. At first, she had protested , but then acquiesced. Truth was, Ned had time on his hands; the census was nearly complete and, as long as he took time to check on nicrophorus americanus each day, he could put the rest of the work on hold.

Gradually, she recovered, and by the week's end she was, again, able to do her full share of the work. Her spirit broken, her body had recovered. It was during this period that they had their first real argument. Ned insisted that he still wanted to help, but she refused and angrily demanded that he go back to his work and leave her alone.

Sensing her fragility and aware of how important her independence was, Ned bowed to her wishes, but he worried and fretted about her constantly. He backed off, but still insisted on preparing supper each night, despite her protests. Ned now spent his nights at the cottage, holding her as she slept. Since he'd moved in, not a single nightmare had interrupted her sleep. She displayed no interest in lovemaking and he didn't press, sensing her body and spirit needed to heal after the emotional battering the revelations had cost her.

Two weeks passed and her spirits seemed to lift, so Ned thought it safe to bring up the subject of Phil Bodington's upcoming visit. Phil and three graduate students were scheduled to arrive on the following Tuesday. When she had first learned of the visit, Addie had been upset, but resigned. She intended to stay at home while he entertained them. At the end of the week, they would be gone. When he broached the subject of her dining with them, she went cold and refused.

He had actually suggested they all eat at the cottage! What was he thinking? Ned had dropped the subject and they went their separate ways for the day, Ned heading for A-5, the last quadrant to be canvassed. He had just begun work in the area, and could have easily completed the census by the week's end, but he was moving slowly until Phil's team arrived. "Hold off a little and give the kids something to do," had been Phil's suggestion, which he had taken up. The students could complete the census. Let them fight their way through the briars. That would still leave time for them to hike around the island, taking a day or two to explore the tidal marshes on the eastern side. Addie had given them permission to go down into the marsh, in fact it had been her suggestion.

While he worried about Addie, Ned looked forward to seeing Phil. He worked hard for the remainder of the week transcribing notes and straightening up the camp. Over the weekend, he laid in a good store of provisions and decided to take Sunday off.

As they sat eating breakfast, he took her hand. "Let's go into the village. Take a ride down the coast. My car still runs, I think."

Addie hesitated, but finally agreed and they spent the day riding through the surrounding countryside and along the coastal roads. They stopped at a roadside stand and ordered fried clams, devouring the succulent clams at an outdoor picnic table overlooking a river. Surrounded by other diners, they watched boats cruise by. To Ned, the warm lassitude of the afternoon was in harmony with the meandering river.

As if reading his thoughts, she gave him a lazy smile. "I haven't had these since I was a teenager."

"Don't talk with your mouth full." They laughed, along with several of their tablemates. She's okay, he thought, as he watched her, eyes full of love. She's going to be okay.

CHAPTER 35

Later, as they crossed the channel in Ned's canoe, the engine putting softly in the cool of the evening, Addie leaned against him and he cradled her in his arms.

She lifted her head, giving him dreamy smile. "Thank you, Mr. Fielding, for this beautiful day, for everything."

"The day isn't over yet."

He kissed her, his hands moving to caress her breasts under her jacket.

"Mmm," she murmured, responding to his embrace. "But, let's not get carried out to sea. I haven't seen Branwen for several weeks and my witchcraft might not be strong enough to save us."

"Tell me about Branwen."

"She's been coming back to the channel for six years now. She's actually a blackfish, or pilot whale, larger than most species of dolphin. She was only a baby when I found her—beached on the west side of the island. Her dead mother lay beside her tangled in an old fisherman's net. Branwen was near death herself. I knew if I released her, she wouldn't survive.

"I pulled her into the water and I brought her around to the cove, holding her at my side. She was limp, but still breathing. I rigged up a small enclosure out of chicken wire and netting to keep her. It was fastened to the dock, very crude, but it did the trick. She was contained and I could care for her.

"I stayed with her, in the pen for nearly a week, leaving only to eat and drink fresh water. I kept a trap submerged by the dock. There was always a fish or two in it and I was able to catch fish from the dock to feed her. Miraculously, she pulled through. I set her free at the end of the second week. I like to think she returns every year, to thank me. Someday, perhaps she'll take us for another ride."

Addie smiled and Ned remembered his dream after the accident.

"The Welsh *Mabinogion*. The myths, that's where you've gotten the names. I've been trying to jog my memory for weeks to figure out where I'd heard them."

"Yes, I love the stories of Mabinogi, especially the four branches. I discovered them quite by accident, through the novels of Evangeline Walton. Do you know her?"

"*Island of the Mighty, Song of Rhiannon*? Yup, I know 'em. My wife, Penny, loved mythology, particularly the Welsh stuff with their emphasis on the power of women, mother succession and all that."

"I found the Walton books, well two anyway, in an old book shop in Derryville, years ago, when I was still married to King. Mr. Granger searched for the other two, and I've collected many versions of the tales since. They're quite unusual. I'm much fonder of them than I am of the Arthur tales."

In front of them, the island loomed, her cliffs shrouded in the early evening fog, the emerald woods peeking up above the mist, the tree tops seeming to grow right out of the clouds. "There is something magical about this place, isn't there?"

"Oh yes, I knew it from the first moment I saw it, on an evening very like this one. It was during our courtship."

"Addie, do you think the associations of the island may still haunt you?"

She shook her head. "I have only happy memories of Winward, even with King. We sailed around the island one evening after eating at a restaurant in Derryville. It's a short sail if the wind is right and we were in a merry, carefree mood.

"He told me the island was for sale, that he was thinking of purchasing it, to preserve it. King was a committed environmentalist, very generous to many conservation groups. In addition to SENCA, he gave to the Audubon Society, the Nature Conservancy, Save the Bay, and many other conservation groups."

Ned listened, somewhat incredulous. A man capable of such generosity, even kindness on the one hand, yet monstrous and sadistic on the other.

"I was thrilled. I had been gushing on about the island, how it was so beautiful and mysterious, when he announced he was thinking of purchasing it. I nearly burst with excitement. After that day, I heard nothing more and forgot about it until just before we were to be married. I overheard some of the locals talking about King's acquisition of Winward Island and his plans for it. I didn't catch all of their words, but I was ecstatic.

"Two days before the wedding, I asked him if what I'd overheard was true. He shrugged and made no comment, so I assumed I'd been mistaken and chided myself for eavesdropping. I thought no more about it until the morning after our wedding night."

She gripped Ned's hand tightly.

"I'd had little sleep and was quite bruised and sore when he burst into my room midmorning and told me to pack a suitcase and prepare for our honeymoon. I stared at him, unable to comprehend. 'Let Sally take care of it then, but do hurry. No fancy clothes, just jeans, that sort of thing.' He made no mention of the previous evening, and I wondered if he even remembered it. I was sexually ignorant, but I had been around drunks before. My uncle had a love affair with the bottle and had often experienced blackouts. King whisked out of the room before I could reply. Not knowing what to do, I did as I was told.

"Before I knew what was happening, we were on Abe Rudder's skiff with our suitcases and several bags of groceries. Abe brought us to the newly-constructed dock on Winward, where a cart awaited us. Abe loaded our things into it and shoved off. He had offered to 'come up and get us settled,' but King shooed him away with 'Honeymoon, Rudder, can't have you along on my honeymoon.'

"We walked up the path onto the cliffs and then through the woods. As we neared the end of the path, just before we were to step into the open, he instructed me to close my eyes. Then, he guided me, blind the rest of the way. When I opened my eyes, the cottage stood before us, just as it looks today—without the barns and all. He'd had it built as a wedding present. Then, he pulled the deed to the eastern half of the island from his pocket. 'When I'm gone, this will be yours, my dear. Windtop will go to the village, but this is for you.'

"The horror of the previous night forgotten for that moment, I threw my arms around him. It was the happiest moment of my marriage, that day in the meadow, my beautiful home staring down at me.

"King was never cruel during our stays on the island. It was as if the island's magic conspired to protect me during the time we spent there.

"As the years went by, we stopped coming out. Once he realized how much I loved it, he used it as weapon. First, he refused to take me there and he would never allow me to go alone. Later, he threatened to change his will and give the entire island away, so that I might never set foot on it again.

"His mind was deteriorating with each passing day. Had he lived a few months longer, I believe he might have carried out his threats and changed the will, but he died, and the island, well half of it, came to me. I've tried to take care of it as best as I'm able, to be deserving of such a wonderful gift."

Ned bent to kiss her forehead as the canoe bumped against the side of the dock. "No one deserves it more than you, my darling. We're home."

That evening, their lovemaking, unlike the fiery passion of earlier days, was slow and gentle. They had undressed each other with gentle caresses as they inched towards the bed, falling in tandem onto soft eiderdowns.

Afterwards, they showered and made love again, then went downstairs to sit by the fire, drinking tea, laughing and talking, the most relaxed they'd been in weeks. As they climbed the stairs, Ned felt his desire rise again, aroused just by brushing against her body, but he held back, afraid she was tired, not wanting to hurt her. As she reached the landing she turned to him, opened her robe and pressed her lovely nakedness against him.

"Oh, Addie," he moaned, pulling her legs up to straddle his hips. "I love you so."

"I know," she whispered, "And I, you."

CHAPTER 36

"So where you going when your divorce is final? Penny's getting the house, right?"

"Don't know yet, Phil. I've got a couple of months to decide."

His boss had been there less than twenty-four hours and already he was mother-henning him. Still, he enjoyed the company of his old friend. He and Phil went back a long way. They had met when undergrads. Both biology majors, they had volunteered to do a study on Narragansett Bay, not unlike the census he was completing on Winward.

Assigned to do the "grunt work," Phil's words, the two of them completed the study, then the graduate students wrote it up, and, as Phil claimed, "grabbed all the glory." Phil had been a senior then, Ned a sophomore. After college, both had gone their separate ways. Phil founded SENCA, while Ned went on to graduate school, but they'd kept in touch.

"You can always come and stay with us. You know Marge would just love to fuss and coo over you. She's always liked you better than me."

"I should be so lucky. Watch out, I might take you up on it."

"Good. Now, where the hell are those three good-for-nothings?"

"Looking for us, Mr. B?" Tim Hollins called from behind them, as three grad students appeared on the path.

Phil and Ned had returned to camp to make lunch for the five of them and thought they were headed towards the group, rather than the opposite. Hollins was tall and thin, a crop of red hair stuck under a worn baseball cap with the SENCA logo stenciled on the front. Clearly, the most competent of the three, he had immediately taken charge. He didn't take any shit from Phil and clearly saw himself as the older man's equal. After all, Phil only had a Master's degree, while he was three quarters of the way through his doctoral program.

"Terms of endearment in the field, m'boy," Phil replied, giving his best W.C. Fields imitation.

"Cut the bullshit, Mr. B. and give us some lunch. We're starving."

"Hold on," Ned said, "We aren't your lackies."

"Please, Dr. Fielding, may we have some lunch?" Hollins made a mock bow.

Wiseass, Ned thought, tossing him the knapsack filled with drinks and sandwiches. "You guys go ahead. I'll be there soon."

Leaving the others, Ned made his way to the cottage, hoping to catch Addie. Disappointed to find her gone, he left a note on the kitchen table. He missed her already. He would be staying at camp all week with the others. The nights would be especially hard.

As he walked back, he thought about the four working with him. Tim Hollins had already irritated him several times in the short time he had been on Winward, declaring Ned's collection methods antiquated, questioning his data, and wondering aloud if the elder man had set up adequate protection for the carrion beetles he had discovered.

Just this morning, Tim had ended a long diatribe with, "I know you're a well-respected researcher, Dr. Fielding, I mean, we've all read your molecular studies, but field work, particularly in this area…well, it's a bit out of your field of expertise, isn't it? Whereas Jack and I have spent the last two years…"

"Cork it, Hollins," Phil had interrupted. "You're out of line. Ned Fielding's field work is without peer."

The younger man had muttered something along the lines of, "We're all scientists. No offense intended," and had said no more, but he clearly intended to conduct his research his way, and would not take orders or direction from anyone. He needn't have worried on that score, as neither Phil nor Ned had egos to match his own. Easygoing and fair, they had always allowed their students free rein—to make their own discoveries as well as their own mistakes.

The other two students, Jack Mason, a short, stocky first year student and Barry Rosen, a thin, speckled young man who looked like a freshman in high school, but was apparently in his third year of graduate studies in marine biology at the University of Rhode Island, were quiet, diligent workers. Unlike Tim Hollins, they seemed to have nothing to prove and appeared to be enjoying their time on the island, both the research and the recreation.

Barry had been recruited as a photographer, to record their field work and observations. His photos would be used for SENCA's records and also for publication in journals, possibly even textbooks. He would also do the web-based work to post findings and research resources for their now-global audience. Together, Barry and Jack made several trips around the island in the canoe. Ned had promised to ask Addie if they might borrow her kayak, which they had spied pulled up on the beach.

As for Addie, she had met them briefly the previous evening and made it clear that she would leave them to their work, if they would accord her the same consideration. When the three students had headed down to the beach for a swim, Phil and Ned had stood together watching her retreat, Aran at her side.

"Interesting woman, buddy. And that coyote's a hoot."

"She has an osprey she's tamed, a dolphin, too, if you can believe it. I've never seen the dolphin, but I've watched the osprey perch on her arm and feed right out her hand. It's incredible."

"I'll say. Probably better to keep that to ourselves," Phil added. "No telling what spin Hollins would put on that kind of information and we don't want him pestering Mrs. Barlow, or writing up some cockamamie story for one of the journals."

"Where'd you find him, anyway? He's a cheeky bastard."

"You haven't seen nothing yet, buddy. Comes from Portsmouth; his Dad's a developer, but he's been really good to SENCA. Goes to Brown, as he has doubtless already informed you. It's usually the first thing out of his mouth when you meet him. Hot to beef up his resume with field credentials. Hadn't had any luck landing a summer position. His dad called me the beginning of June and asked if I'd take him on. He's not a bad sort, just a bit of a jerk. I guess he had trouble getting professors to recommend him for the projects he was interested in. Are we surprised?

"He's been driving Marty crazy, but he's done great work out at Tunamessett, marking the new trails, collecting data. Believe it or not, he's great with kids. He got the camp program going, runs the workshops, and trains counselors. As you can see, he's a take-charge kind of guy. That's what we needed.

"So tell me, buddy. Is that the last we'll see of the mysterious Mrs. Barlow?"

"Probably." Ned hesitated, then decided to confide in his friend. "I'm involved with her, Phil."

"No, you mean romantically?"

"Yup."

"Hey, you move fast, buddy. Does Penny know about this?"

"No, and I'd rather you didn't mention it. Not that it matters."

"Seriously?"

"Yup."

"So, how'd this all happen?"

"Well, you knew about her helping me, saving my life, during the storm. Things just sort of went on from there. It's a little scary, if you want to know the truth. I've never felt this way about a woman before, even in the early days with Penny."

"So?"

"So, I don't know. I haven't said anything about any of this to Ned or Syd, so please don't tell anyone. I know Marge still bumps into Penny. So please tell her mum's the word. In November, we sign the divorce papers; I'll see the kids then and tell 'em about Addie. Janie and Ned are getting married, you know. I'm going to be a grandfather by this time next year. Pretty amazing, huh?"

"Hey, congratulations, Gramps!" Phil winked at him. "I expect the lovely Mrs. Barlow will keep you young. Come on, let's go round up the whippersnappers."

CHAPTER 37

The week flew by. Four completed work that would have taken Ned weeks. Overweight and out of shape, Phil tired easily and took a nap every afternoon, but Ned and the students worked from sun-up until close to dusk. Barry's Nikon recorded nearly every move they made. They had been so productive that, by the week's end, Phil was threatening to cut short Ned's stay. He was teasing. With the fall migration only a few weeks away, there was still plenty of work to be done.

Addie had responded graciously to his note. Of course, the men could use the kayak. She would leave the paddle inside it in the morning, or Ned could collect it from the shed. She stopped by briefly on two occasions with baskets laden with vegetables and fish one night and lobsters another. She stayed only a minute both times. The second time, Ned was away and she found Phil alone at the camp, resting in the canvas chair.

"Hello, Mrs. Barlow."

Phil jumped up to offer her the seat.

She smiled shyly and declined his offer to sit. Although she was not inclined to linger, Phil Bodington seemed a warm, friendly soul and she felt comfortable in his presence. She found it hard to believe that the stocky man with the bald pate of graying hair was only two years older than Ned. Ned's sandy hair, thick and tousled with curls, hadn't a hint of gray and his body was lean and trim, and he was in better shape than the college students with whom he worked. Of course, she mused, she'd had little experience studying men's physiques. While her husband had been a handsome man, King had been overweight and flaccid and looked every one of his fifty-five years when they had married.

Phil slipped a faded blue work shirt over his bare, white hairless chest, and added, "How 'bout a cool drink? Ned and the others should be back soon."

"Thank you, but I really do have to get back."

She handed him the heavy basket, which he set down immediately, marveling to himself at her strength. Striking, she was. Not gorgeous, but handsome, even if a bit remote and inscrutable. Lovely when she smiled.

"Sure you won't stay?"

She shook her head, smiling shyly.

"Well, thank you. The bluefish the other night was delicious and now lobsters. You're spoiling us!"

As she turned to go, he approached her, hand outstretched, "Mrs. Barlow, if I don't see you again, thank you for your kindness, for the use of the dock, for all this delicious food, for everything."

Hesitating, she then took his hand. "My pleasure, Mr. Bodington. After so many years, it has been a nice change to have Ned, Mr. Fielding, here."

For a moment, Phil thought she meant to say more and he waited, expectantly.

"Well, I'll be off then."

Phil touched her shoulder lightly, restraining her for an instant. "I knew King, Mrs. Barlow. He was very generous to us, don't get me wrong, but I...What I mean to say is, Ned's told me that you two have been seeing something of each other. Not my business, of course, but I just wanted to say, I'm glad. Glad for Ned as he's my closest friend and he deserves to be happy. I'm also glad for you, my dear. Life with King can't have been easy and you've been alone here a long time."

"Did Ned tell you about my husband?"

"Never mentioned him, although he's talked about you, all good things, I assure you. I wouldn't say anything to Ned about King either. Let the dead rest in peace. Just glad you two are together's all I'm saying."

"Thank you."

She touched his arm lightly as she turned away, but not before Phil saw that her eyes brimmed with tears. He wondered if he should have spoken. How anyone as gentle and kind as she, could have ended up with that bastard is beyond me, he thought, settling back down in the chair, a cold beer in hand.

Ned returned a short time later, terribly disappointed at having missed her. Phil decided to say nothing about King Barlow. Let his widow tell Ned in her own time. Perhaps she already had. Anyway, it wasn't his business.

After the meal, they sat up until after midnight chatting, the lanterns glowing, the night warm and filled with stars. One by one they retired, Tim, Jack and Barry to their state-of-the art domed tent thirty feet away, the two men into Ned's tattered canvas tent. He'd had the tent since his own graduate days and he couldn't bear to exchange it for a new sleek nylon one. Phil had brought his own cot.

Screams wakened them all, just before dawn. Barry's voice shouted outside the tent as Ned rose and pulled back the flap. "Dr. Fielding, we've gotta help. Must be Mrs. Barlow."

"Jesus Christ," Tim yelled behind him, as more screams reached them. "What the hell? Where're the flashlights?"

"Hold on, slow down everyone," Ned said. "Stay calm. It's all right."

"Sounds like she's in trouble, buddy. Don't you think we'd better go have a look?"

"It's a nightmare, Phil."

"You sure?" Hollins, skeptical as always, had found his flashlight and was fumbling with his shoes. "People don't usually scream that loud when they have nightmares."

"She's okay, truly. It's not as bad as it sounds. Sound carries on the island. She's fine."

"You know best," Phil said, wondering if the nightmares had anything to do with King Barlow.

"But how does he know?"

"Go back to bed, Hollins. Party's over," Phil barked.

His friend's sharp tone surprised Ned, but he said a silent thank you to him for intervening.

"Guess all those rumors are true," Jack said, as they turned away and headed for their tent.

"What are you talking about?"

"You know. 'Bout the Widow. That's what they call her in town you know. Say she's a witch. Rumor has it she did away with her husband."

"Who have you been listening to, Mason? Abe Rudder's half-cocked stories? He's the biggest gossip this side of the Atlantic."

"It's not just Mr. Rudder. Everyone talks like that about her," Tim said. "You have to admit, she is kind of strange."

"I think she's nice," Barry said. "And beautiful too. She must be really lonely all by herself out here. And, she sure has been nice to us, all the food."

"How would you know if she's nice or not? You've barely seen her and I don't believe she even looked at you that first day when we met her."

"I've watched her, with the animals. And I talked to her, the day you guys were out in the kayak. She showed me her garden, in fact. She's incredible, what she's got growing there."

"All right, enough is enough," Phil interrupted, afraid that Barry would elaborate about the osprey, or worse, the dolphin. "Mrs. Barlow has been a gracious host to whom we should all (he looked straight at Tim) be very grateful. None of us here believes that garbage about her being a witch or any of it. It's just small town gossip.

"Now, we've got a long hard last day ahead of us, so let's try and get a little more sleep." The first rays of the sun peeked over the woods to the east as the three young men headed to the beach for a swim. Ned and Phil lay on their cots, silent but awake.

Finally Phil spoke, "She's had a rough time of it, I expect."

"Yup."

"Know much about the trial, inquest, whatever it was?"

"No, do you?"

"Only what I read at the time. Of course, Barlow's lawyer was in touch, about his gift. The island I mean. I knew King though."

"How?"

"We go back a few years, through his gifts to SENCA. Met his first wife, Janet, years ago. Mousy, unassuming type. I'd never met Adelaide, though I'd seen her photograph."

"What did you think of him?"

"Oh, I liked him well enough, at first. Everybody did. He was very generous to us. His money funded a great many projects over the years. In later years, I found him to be, well, he was a bastard. No polite way of sayin' it. Call it senility, insanity, whatever you want, but in the last years of his life, he was crazy. Mean, ugly, and ruthless to those who got in his way."

"But, how did you?"

"According to local gossip, the last year of his life, Barlow's festering rage turned full force on his wife. He told wild stories of her infidelities, impropriety, and all kinds of nonsense to anyone who would listen. His own lawyer assured me that none of it was true. I never met your Mrs. Barlow, before this week, but I sure pitied her. King was on the phone almost daily, changing the terms of his bequest, telling me SENCA was to have the whole island one minute, none of it the next.

"After a while, I stopped returning his calls. Figured nothing was that important that I had to put up with his shit. Then he died and folks had a field day. The rumor mongers tried to pin it on her. Who knows what really happened that night, but who cares? If she killed him, or left him to die as they said, probably had a good reason."

She did, Ned thought, but said nothing, too overcome with worry and fatigue to speak. Addie hadn't had a nightmare for weeks. Now, without him there holding her and protecting her, the terrors had returned.

CHAPTER 38

Ned watched as Rufus pushed off and ferried Phil and the young men away from the island. He was sorry to see them go. He would miss Phil's company. At the same time, he was anxious to find Addie. He searched the island for her the morning they had awoken to her screams, but she seemed to be avoiding him. He left messages for her at the cottage and in her mail chest. "See you tomorrow night. Don't worry. Love, A," was her only response.

Their last evening, the men had feasted on steamers and corn from the stands in the village and Ned had surprised them, even Hollins, by serving a savory mash made from the roots of silverweed, the yellow flowers that covered the cliffs. The night had been quiet and the dawn held not a trace of breeze. "Bet there's a storm coming," Phil predicted as they hiked down to the dock.

"No way," Hollins called over his shoulder.

"Always the know-it-all," Phil said in a low voice as he slowed his pace to put the others out of earshot. "So, buddy, let me know how things turn out. Be careful, okay? Your Mrs. Barlow, well she's all that Barry said, and then some I expect, but I'd take it slow. I don't believe all that crap. You know that, but I'd make sure of what I was getting myself into."

"Phil."

"Sorry, end of lecture. Let me know if you need anything—and count on us if you need a place to stay when you return."

"Thanks. I may take you up on it. At least for a couple of weeks in November."

"Terrific."

"Phil, where was the trial, inquest, whatever held? Do you know?"

"Why?"

"Just curious."

"Derryville, I think. I'd leave it alone if I were you. What happened twelve years ago is ancient history. Besides, you know how accurate the newspapers are!"

"Just wondered, that's all."

"We'll send you copies of all Barry's pictures. Took about twenty-five rolls."

"Great."

"Take care, buddy."

"You, too. Remember, three miles a day." Ned smiled, hugging his friend. He had dragged Phil for a forty-five minute walk every day for the past week, extolling the virtues of regular exercise to his sedentary friend. "And give my love to Marge."

"Will do. Thank Mrs. Barlow again for us."

Turning away as the boat rounded the point, Ned headed for camp. He intended to spend the day taking stock, cleaning up, organizing his notes of the past week's work and checking on the buried carcasses. Some of the young were due to hatch any day.

It began to rain two hours later, a light sprinkle that turned into a torrential downpour, lasting well into the evening.

CHAPTER 39

The day after Phil's departure, Ned broke up his camp, stored the tents and other gear in Addie's barn, and moved into the cottage. Addie had suggested such a move weeks earlier, but he had held off, wanting to wait until after the men's visit. Addie cleared a work space in the near shed for his files and specimens. The rest of his gear he stored in the barn. The census was nearly completed and his notes were current. With the study winding down, Ned fell into the routine of the farm, helping when she needed him. He found that he enjoyed the work and the quiet rhythm of their days.

Mechanically inclined, he worked on the old tractor and rebuilt the engine of Addie's outboard, which had been broken for nearly two years.

"I'd have learned to fix it someday," she told him, before thanking him profusely.

On off days, Ned rode up and down the coast, scouring junk yards for replacement parts for the farm's generator, which had also been out of commission for several years. He gardened, fished and helped with the basket deliveries, the latter job eventually becoming his alone as Addie was only too glad to avoid the trip into town.

One late afternoon run, Abe Rudder watched Ned loading up for the run across the channel. "Now, yer doin' her work, Fielding. Bewitched fer sure?"

The Widow's reputation had softened since news of Ned's rescue had gotten around. Folks treated her more charitably, even Abe. Still, the elder Rudder still did not approve of their liaison. The whole town was abuzz with it, but aside from Abe, no one commented on the relationship in Ned's presence.

At first, he wondered how people had found out with such alacrity, but Rufus had set him straight on that score. "Mr. Fielding, how do you think folks around here get their jollies? Geez, just go into any house along the water, all of 'em got them big, high powered telescopes. And you don't 'spose they're bird-watchin' with 'em, do ya?"

Ned loaded the last of the provisions into the boat. "Cut the crap, Abe. That's bullshit, and you know it. She's no more a witch than you are."

"Just kiddin, son. Geez, yer touchy today, ain't ya? Have a lovers' spat or somethin'?"

Ned's eyes flashed fire, and he readied to do battle. Fortunately, Rufus interrupted the stand-off. "Package fer you, Mr. F. Came after the regular mail delivery. Thought it might be important."

"Thanks Rufus."

Ned grabbed the padded manila folder and shoved off without a glance at the elder Rudder.

"Mark my words," Abe shouted. "This business will come to no good. Better watch yerself!"

Furious, Ned opened the throttle and wove dangerously close to several boats moored in the harbor as he headed out into the channel. When he reached the mouth of the harbor, he slowed down, feeling foolish. Why had he reacted to Abe that way? Get a grip, Ned. Get a goddamn grip.

Since Phil's visit, curiosity about Addie's past had haunted him, but since he did not wish to cause her pain, he hadn't broached the subject. Somehow, when alone, however, he could not let it go. His curiosity about King Barlow's death ate away at him, especially since Addie refused to discuss it. It was none of his business, of course, but he still felt he had to know. He resolved to pay a visit to the Derryville Library, when time allowed it. Perhaps old newspaper accounts would give him the answers he sought.

He tied up at the dock and unloaded the provisions, tossing them into the garden cart. Midway through his task, he spotted the package Rufus had handed him, lying where he had tossed it in his fit of pique before shoving off. He sat on Addie's mail chest and tore open the package. A scribbled note from Phil lay atop a pile of smaller manila envelopes enclosed within the large mailer:

"Buddy,

Thought you'd like these. Barry outdid himself, don't you think? I've let Hollins loose on the media. He's writing a couple of articles—one for the *Providence Journal*, another for the *Globe*, and a 'serious one'—Hollin's Words—for the *Quarterly*. Hope the *Q* article won't launch an invasion of your little paradise. Next year, I doubt we'll be able to keep them away. Poor Mrs. B. Tell her we're sorry. Nicrophorus americanus is just too important to keep under wraps. Regards to her.
Phil"

Opening the top folder, Ned found the first set of black and white photographs. Taken on the first day of their visit, there were shots of all four men, the arrival, settling in and exploring the area around Ned's camp. Hollins was clearly in charge, playing up to the camera in almost every shot. Ned chuckled as he leafed through the stack. A cursory glance revealed that the packets were arranged in chronological order. As he flipped through each envelope's contents, he marveled at Barry's skill and perceptions.

The field shots were magnificent, close-ups of nicrophorus americanus, their egg clusters and the hatching witnessed by Barry and Jack early the last morning of their visit. Hollins, who was taking a last minute survey, had been devastated to have missed it. Phil was right. Once these photographs hit the *Quarterly* the island would be invaded. No way to stop it.

There was an additional packet attached at the back, the words, "for Mr. Fielding," scribbled across it in Barry's hand. Ned opened the envelope and shook the photos out. Some were black and white, and the rest vivid color prints, taken from various spots on the island. Early morning shots, photos taken at sunset, the colors vibrant, almost pulsating. Almost every shot was of Addie, some from a distance, others close up. He wondered as he flipped through the stack if she had been aware of Barry's presence. This question was answered as he came to a picture where she stood facing the camera, smiling.

He had caught her on the dock, returning from pulling the lobster pots, two heavy burlap bags at her side. She was headed for the holding pots at the end of the dock and she wore a sleeveless white tee shirt under her overalls. Barry had captured her strength, the strong beautiful arms rippled with muscle under her load, the slender body, erect and proud. The next photo was even more surprising. It showed Addie, crouched beside an open bag, holding a huge lobster, claws splayed, looking up at the camera, smiling again.

Ned remembered Barry's words, but had never thought to ask him or Addie later on if they had ever met. Obviously, they had. Feelings of jealousy and possessiveness crept over him for an instant, and he suddenly felt irritated that she hadn't told him about meeting Barry. Why should she though?

There were other pictures of her taken from a distance as she paddled in the kayak, rode the tractor through the open fields, and walked along the cliffs at dusk. These photos, Ned was relatively certain had been taken without her knowledge. A haunting shot of her perched at the edge of the cliffs on the northeast point of the island made him shudder. Her eyes were deeply troubled, her face lined with fatigue and sorrow and he wondered if this shot had been taken the morning after the nightmare. In their time together she had obviously held back, not allowing him to glimpse the depths of her despair, but here, when she thought herself alone, she'd let down her guard. Here her face was an open book, the look of despondency and hopelessness reflected there made Ned shudder. The picture had been taken from a great distance using a powerful zoom lens, but it captured her pain with startling clarity.

Worry and concern furrowed his brow as Ned tucked the photographs away, finished loading the cart, and set off for the cottage. Why wouldn't she tell him about her husband's death? What had happened that night twelve years ago? If he was to help her heal, he felt certain that knowing what happened that night was crucial.

CHAPTER 40

"Where are you off to so bright and early?"

Addie leaned on one elbow, the sheet pulled back revealing one breast, her hair trailing over the bedclothes in soft profusion; a beautiful smile lit up her face. It was seldom that he arose before her, but he needed to get out before sunrise to spot the migrating birds.

Resisting the powerful urge to shed his clothes and slip back into bed, he kissed her lightly.

"Work, my love." He fondled her breast, and she drew her arms around his neck, caressing and stroking. Her kisses, light and whispering, covered his neck and his chest. His unbuttoned shirt slipped off as she drew him nearer.

"Addie."

"Mmm." Her hand stroked his erection, straining against his khaki field shorts. "Just stay a few minutes, please."

His hands reached under the covers. Unable to resist the feel of her skin, Ned sighed as her soft, round breasts pressed against his bare chest, long legs encircling his waist. Her hands slipped into his shorts and together they unfastened his fly. In one movement, their bodies joined. As Ned entered her, she cried out with pleasure, taking him deeper and deeper with every thrust of her slender hips.

Afterwards, they lay still, Addie astride him, breathing evenly, almost asleep. He nibbled at her ear. "Addie, my darling, I have to go."

"Mmm."

"Now. I'm sorry," He gently rolled her to his side and withdrew himself from the warm recesses. She nestled beside him, arms massaging his chest. Kissing her deeply, he drew her close for one moment more, then pulled away and hopped out of bed. Covering her warm naked body against the chill of the early morning, he threw on his clothes.

Chiding himself for missing the sunrise, he grabbed his shoes. Already the second week of October, their time together was growing shorter. Acutely conscious of the uncertainty of his future, their future, he shook himself. No time to consider that now.

"I'm going into town this morning. Need anything?"

"No, why? We just got supplies."

"I have a bunch of things I forgot and I need to make phone calls."

"You can use the phone here."

"I know, but I've gotta go into Derryville, to the library. I need a couple of references and I can use their computer."

Ned hated lying, had never lied to Addie, but how could he tell her the real purpose for his trip? How could he tell her that he was going to check up on her? To research her husband's death and nose around where he didn't belong, hoping to discover through the accounts of strangers what had really happened the night King Barlow died. What role had his beloved Addie played in the death of her abusive husband? The thought was inconceivable, but still, he had to know for certain.

He had gone back and forth about the trip. One day he would tell himself it was stupid, unnecessary, and an outrageous betrayal of a woman who had given him nothing but kindness and love. The next day, he would convince himself that he could never be happy with Addie unless he knew the truth. Finally, sick of worrying and fretting, he resolved to go, to put the whole business behind him, and to get it out of his system.

"You can use my laptop."

"I need two specific databases, my love. Most libraries have them."

"Maybe I'll come with you."

"It'd be boring, all that sitting around while I make notes."

"Ned, is something the matter?"

"No, why?" Regarding her expression, he knew with certainty that she saw through the lie. "I just need to do this and I'd rather be—"

"Alone?" She forced a smile.

"No, that's not it at all. Of course, if you want to come, we'll go together."

"No, go. I'm fine. I have too much to do anyway. Not a good day for me to take off. Now, hurry or you'll even miss the gulls."

Guilty, but resigned, Ned set off for the makeshift blind he had erected on the western cliffs. Over the previous months, he had built a number of crude concealments, mostly piles of brush thrown over a frame of poles, scattered around the island, but the beach blind was the most advantageous spot to bird watch in the early morning. Often, he counted hundreds of brant, geese and all manner of water fowl, the flocks bobbing in the early morning surf. When the sun rose, they moved on, their journey just beginning.

A thick fog crept in, obscuring his view. By the time he reached the blind, the whole area was blanketed in a pea soup. Visibility was only about two feet in front of him. No bird watching this morning, no counting, no note taking. Whatever birds bobbed on the outskirts of Winward would reach southern climes without his observing or counting them.

"Shit," he muttered aloud, sitting down hard on the blind's plank bench. Another wasted morning.

Chapter 41

Hand on hip, the diminutive librarian in heather wool skirt and matching cardigan, smiled at Ned. "You're welcome to use any of the computers, Mr. Fielding, but we also have the actual newspaper clippings, if you can believe it. They're kept in the warehouse across the street." She squinted at him over thick bi-focals. "Would you like me to find someone to let you in?"

Ned was unsure whether or not to scrap his snooping project, when she added, "You know, you'd have much better luck over at the *Courier*."

Thanking her, Ned exited the one-story brick building, immediately drawn by the smell of hamburgers cooking. He remembered that he had not eaten since the previous evening. He had left the cottage that morning in such a hurry, he had forgotten breakfast.

Following the scent, he soon came upon the Sparkle Diner. He sat in a wooden-sided booth, back to the counter. When Betsy, the friendly waitress with tight ginger curls and a yellow striped uniform that fit her curvaceous frame as if it had been spray painted on, arrived, Ned ordered a chorizo roll, onion rings and a milk shake.

"Sure thing, sweetheart."

Betsy disappeared, leaving him to gaze out the somewhat grimy picture window. Derryville Center consisted of the library, attached to the town hall, a few shops, the Sparkle Diner and a strip of three gas stations with attached convenience stores. A massive three-story inn sat at the top of Main Street, its windows broken and boarded up. The flower beds surrounding it had long since given way to three-foot weeds. The picture windows of the inn's restaurant had once afforded wide, unobstructed ocean views.

After lunch, Ned stopped beside the inn's front door to read the restaurant menu, still tacked inside a glass case. They had served mostly seafood, a few steaks thrown in for landlubbers. He walked completely around the imposing, shingled structure, admiring its turrets, wide veranda and domed cupola. "What a great place," he had said aloud, unaware that an elderly man, in overalls and oilskin coat, gray wisps of hair poking out from a faded blue baseball cap watched from the shadows to one side of the building. They struck up a conversation and in a few minutes, he had learned a fair bit of local history, specifically that which concerned the demise of the Breakwater Inn. "Some show biz type bought it last, thinkin' of turnin' it into a night club. Can you imagine?" Ned couldn't. As they spoke, Ned realized that he had no idea where the newspaper office was located.

"'Bout a mile south of here," his companion pointed. "Take the coast road—straight on north to Marsh Pond Road. There's a right turn there. I think there's a sign—just go straight on, it's not far. Can't miss it…long, low building, nothing much else on Marsh Road."

Ned thanked the man and bid him goodbye. A short time later, he was settled in the conference room of the *Derryville Courier*, a stack of old newspapers beside him on the huge mahogany conference table.

"Close at five, take your time," Miss Brigham, a sprightly receptionist in her mid thirties, blonde hair swept up in an elaborate chignon, had informed him. She was new at the paper and had never heard of King Barlow or the circumstances surrounding his death, but it didn't take her long to dig up the issues in question. She also brought in another stack. "Not sure if you want these. They're not about his death, but the man was written up a good bit. I didn't go too far back, six years maybe, but there are some wedding pictures and other stuff. Want to take a look?"

"Yes, thank you." Ned smiled up at her, reading glasses perched on the end of his nose. She left him alone and closed the door softly behind her.

He glanced at the top of the second stack and found an announcement of King Barlow's engagement to Adelaide Leech, daughter of the late Calvin and Marybeth Leech of Newport, ward of Mildred and Weston McCulley of Derryville. No picture. Skipping through the stack, he skimmed the articles concerning various charity benefits made possible through the generosity of "The King" as well as several articles extolling his unwavering support of local conservation groups. Impatient to read information directly relating to the man's demise, Ned put the remainder of the stack aside.

The two-column obituary listed a dizzying array of charities to which the deceased had contributed. Ned tossed it aside. Jesus Christ, he thought, his hand already black with newsprint ink. Was the man a saint or a monster? He began reading article after article about King Barlow's death.

King Barlow found dead by young wife.

Young wife a widow already.

Wealthy philanthropist, conservationist and dedicated environmentalist, struck down in the prime of life.

Who will take the King's place?

All the news accounts stated that the deceased had been discovered in the early dawn hours by his much younger wife of five years. By all accounts, he had died in the middle of the night, around 2 a.m., but his body had not been discovered until the following morning. Mrs. Barlow was indisposed and not taking calls, but several enterprising photographers had snapped her on the grounds of Windtop from some distance away. The grainy photos both showed a thin, wraith, one gust of wind enough to carry her away. In one, she walked what looked to be a black cocker spaniel on a huge expanse of lawn. In the other, she strolled alone along a tree-lined drive. Her hair was shoulder length, loose and blowing, her face a blur in both pictures.

Digging deeper in the stack, he finally found the articles he sought.

Inquest ordered in the Barlow death.

Was she to blame?

The young Mrs. Barlow to testify at the inquest.

There were several more, the headlines becoming more pointed and accusatory as the inquest drew near.

Did she let him die?

Teenage bride to testify.

Why didn't she call the doctor?

Did she wait too long?

The King's heart medicine in easy reach in the bedroom; could she have saved him? Was the King's death an accident or murder?

King left to die while the girl looked on.

The King's widow to answer for his death.

Ned read through each article, incredulous that a newspaper would publish such rubbish. Much of what he read appeared to be gossip and wild speculation and the accounts of the inquest were no better. No transcripts were furnished, just more of the same speculations and doubts. There were several fuzzy photographs of Addie on the arm of a tall, thin blond man, her attorney, Jim Talbot, according to the caption. Her head was bowed and she looked away from the camera, one hand gripping Talbot's sleeve, as if hanging on for dear life.

The cause of death had been established early on, a massive heart attack. While King Barlow had died of natural causes, the inquest had come about to investigate possible negligence on his widow's part. According to the medical examiner, the heart attack had not killed King Barlow instantly. He had apparently had sexual relations shortly before he was stricken. His wife was to be called in to give an account of herself.

The impending inquiry spawned a host of lurid speculations, all printed in the *Courier,* concerning the stresses and strains of sexually satisfying a much younger wife. King's heart medication was, according to the investigator, ten feet away on his dresser. The prescription had been filled that morning by the housekeeper, Sally Mendoza. Why hadn't his wife brought it to him?

Addie testified that she had indeed had intimate relations with her husband that evening, but that she had then retired to her own room and left her husband sleeping in his bedroom. When questioned about this, she spoke the truth, "My husband has always insisted on separate bedrooms. He does not, did not, like his sleep disturbed."

He was generally an early riser. When she had risen the following morning and not found him downstairs, she had gone to his room and discovered the body. Her testimony was corroborated by the housekeeper, Mrs. Mendoza. It had been Sally who had phoned the doctor and the police. In the face of these accounts and no evidence to support a different scenario, the inquest ruled that King Barlow died of natural causes.

Legally, the matter was put to rest, but the papers kept the story alive for several more weeks. Three weeks after his death, a retrospective of his life, complete with two page spread of photographs and several articles, was published. It appeared that the anniversary of his death continued to be marked for six years after the fact with the same tired photos dredged up and reprinted.

Photos of the first Mrs. Barlow reminded Ned of Mamie Eisenhower. She seemed much better suited to her portly, round-faced husband, than the slender wisp of a girl that succeeded her. Ned stared at Addie's wedding photographs for a long time, suspended in a swirling torrent of questions. The musty smell of old newsprint filled his sinuses and he felt a headache coming on.

Her appearance hadn't changed very much. Her hair was shorter and her body perhaps a little thinner, but the lovely lines of her figure were evident, despite layers of organdy and lace. In one picture, her husband gazed down at her, lascivious hunger in his wild, dark eyes. Ned felt a stab of fury and helpless rage, knowing what lay ahead for the shy, smiling bride, who stared up at her husband with what appeared to be trust and happiness in her eyes.

The most remarkable thing about the pictures was her eyes. The eyes in these photographs were those of a stranger. This girl's eyes laughed, twinkling mischievously as she smiled for the photographer. Her look was direct, confident and happy.

Ned thought of her eyes now, haunted even in laughter, guarded and watchful, except during their lovemaking. Then, she would either close them or fix them on him with such a look of love, it brought tears to his eyes. Her eyes held such pain, even when they smiled, that it sometimes hurt Ned to look into them. In contrast, this girl seemed to have not a care in the world. Lovely as they were, he thought, the eyes in the photograph seemed almost shallow in comparison. He set the paper aside.

"Excuse me, Mr. Fielding. We're closing." Ned jumped, startled by the sudden appearance of Miss Brigham. "Oh, I am sorry."

"My fault. Didn't hear you come in. I apologize for staying so long. Is it really five?"

"Close to it."

Thanking her, he gathered the papers, then rushed to his car. It would be dark by the time he reached the island and he had done none of the errands he had lied about. Shit, he thought, racing along the coast road.

All the shops were closed when he reached the village. He would return to the island empty-handed. He prayed Abe was still around, as he needed to fill the boat's gas tank.

The Pickle Shack was closed, no sign of the Rudders. Ned grabbed his empty gas tanks and drove two miles back along the coast road to the nearest open station, cursing himself for being so stupid. Darkness enveloped him as he made his way towards Cook's Channel a half hour later, weaving carefully around the many boats still moored in the harbor.

He spent the entire trip across the channel formulating an elaborate series of excuses before finally deciding, as he tied up at the dock, that he would tell Addie the truth. She'll understand, he told himself, not very convincingly. No matter, he was unwilling to lie any further.

She was waiting on the porch, his long tattered gray cardigan wrapped around her against the cool fall evening. She waved and he smiled, waving back as he advanced into her outstretched arms.

"Where have you been? I was just about to set off for the village. We were worried."

"I'm sorry, my darling."

Ned scooped her up and carried her into the cottage, Aran at their heels. "Can I tell you about it over dinner? I'm starving."

CHAPTER 42

"So?"

Ned looked up at her, a spoonful of delicious fall vegetable soup in his hand. Addie had served it with cornmeal and molasses bread, and a spinach salad tossed with peppery radishes.

She looked especially lovely, he thought, as he reached out to take her hand. She was dressed in jeans and a blue turtleneck, now that autumn nights had become chilly. She wore no brassiere and almost never did, unless she was going to town. Her nipples stood erect and perfect, clearly visible under the soft blue fabric. He longed to cup the soft, round breasts and kiss her full, beautiful lips. He craved her warmth as an antidote to the guilt of his day of deceit, craved the blissful escape of their lovemaking to erase his shame. Her hair fell soft and lustrous over her shoulders and down her back. She preferred it braided, but knew that he loved her to wear it down. This obvious effort to please him, made Ned feel even worse and he hung his head, wondering how to explain.

"Ned, what's wrong?"

She startled him and Ned jumped, catching the end of his soup spoon just as it slipped from the table.

"Nothing. Oh, sorry."

"Tell me about your day. What's the big mystery?" She smiled at him, eyes, innocent and trusting.

"Addie, I don't exactly know how to tell you this, so I'm just going to come out and say it. I don't want to lie to you and I did this morning. It made me feel awful and I won't ever do it again."

Worry spread over her face as Ned forced himself to go on. "I didn't go to town to do errands. And I didn't go to find research resources at the Derryville Library. In fact, I spent hardly any time at the library. My whole afternoon was spent going through old *Derryville Couriers*, the ones from the time of your husband's death."

"But why?"

"I don't know exactly. I just had to know. You've always been so reluctant to talk about it."

"Why?" She repeated absently, her face a mask of confusion and hurt.

"I thought I should know the truth, so that I could help you, if you ever—"

She rose from the table, voice tremulous with emotion. "And you think the newspapers tell the truth?"

"Addie, I'm sorry. It was stupid. It's none of my business. I'm sorry I didn't tell you the truth. I was afraid you'd be angry and wouldn't want me to go."

Angry tears rimmed her eyes. "So you wanted all the sordid details on the murdering widow?"

"Addie!"

"No, Ned. Leave me alone!"

She slammed out the front door of the cottage and ran through the fields towards the northern cliffs. Ned wanted to follow, but stopped himself, respecting her need to be alone.

He waited all night on the porch, but she did not return until shortly after sunrise.

"I'm all right," was all she said.

As he rose to embrace her, she held up her hand to stop him. Although wild and disheveled in appearance, her demeanor was calm, almost peaceful. Holding him at arm's length, she brushed past him into the house.

"I need to sleep, Ned. Can we please talk later?"

He let her go and followed her into the house.

She went up to the bedroom and closed the door softly, but firmly behind her. Ned curled up on the living room couch, the worn, tawny linen of its cushions cool against his face. He awoke sometime later, disoriented and groggy, to sounds of her working in the kitchen. She stood at the sink, a red checked apron tied around her slim waist, washing their supper dishes. She had showered and changed into a soft green turtleneck and grey sweatpants. Her hair hung damp and loose down her back.

Crossing the room, Ned gently put his arms around her, nuzzling the back of her neck. "I'm sorry, Addie. I love you so much." Tears stung his eyes as he felt her back stiffen. "I would never do anything to hurt you. I don't know why, well, I do know why I did what I did yesterday, but I'm so very, very sorry, my sweet, darling." He pressed against the warmth of her back, his head buried in her hair, damp and smelling of coconut.

She continued her washing until all the glasses and plates had been placed to dry in the wooden dish rack beside the sink. The flatware she dried by hand and returned them to the wooden box beside the sink. Only then did she turn to face him, her slender arms circling his neck.

"There is nothing to forgive." She gazed up, her eyes sad, but resigned. "I don't blame you at all for wanting to know. I should have, would have told you myself… about King's death, if I could. You see, I have no recollection of that night."

"But you testified," he blurted out, forgetting his resolve never to bring up what he'd learned from his reading.

"Jim and I worked on that together." She took his hand and led him into the living room. They sat together on the couch, hands still entwined. "Jim Talbot, my lawyer, thought it would be better if I said something, rather than 'I don't remember.' And of course, Sally, Mrs. Mendoza said the same thing."

"The housekeeper?"

She nodded. "I don't believe Sally ever liked me. She certainly didn't help much over the years, when King, well, you know, but, in the end, she did help me a little. I'm not sure just how Jim got her to do it, but she did."

"You remember nothing?"

"Nothing from the time we finished dinner until the next morning. We'd had a quarrel. Or rather, King yelled. Rather than enduring his threats in silence, I responded.

"He was raving, very drunk as usual, and going on and on about how I'd never set foot on Winward again. The first years of our marriage, we had spent quite a lot of time on the island, weekends, summer, many days just sailing out for a picnic, but as the years passed by, he would punish me by ceasing our island visits. He knew I was happy here, gardening, walking, exploring, much happier than I ever was at Windtop.

"Windtop was a beautiful house. It had lovely formal gardens and the furnishings were exquisite. But, for all its splendor, it was a cold and lonely place. Perhaps it was just that I was so unhappy there that it seemed so dismal and unfriendly. Here, I came alive and felt at home.

"Anyway, that evening, he was once again threatening to change his will, and I acquiesced. While I was heartbroken, I held up my head and told him that he owed me nothing and that I could make my own way. I said that the island was his to give away and that I did not need his charity. This enraged him. The last thing I remember is him coming at me and ripping at my clothes.

"Then, it was morning and I was in my own bed. My head throbbed with pain. I had a large lump at the base of my skull—so I assumed that King had knocked me out. It wasn't the first time. I assumed he had somehow managed to carry me to my bed. Then the doctor arrived and told me he was dead.

"I never saw the dress I'd been wearing that night. It vanished. I've always assumed King ripped it beyond repair and that Sally simply disposed of it. When I asked her about it at the time, she just shrugged and would say nothing. If she knew anything about the previous night, she wasn't talking and no amount of coaxing on my part could draw it out of her.

"Later on, when I pressed her, she said the doctor had ordered her to say nothing. So I asked Dr. Bickford myself. He also refused to tell me anything. Said things were better left alone. He told me, 'Best forget it Adelaide. Let the King rest in peace, without airing a lot of dirty laundry.' I pleaded with him, but to no avail. He refused to elaborate.

"That's when the nightmares began." She smiled ruefully, her hand reaching up to stroke his cheek.

"From remembering?"

"No, the opposite. Somehow, I know I was there when King died, but I can't remember. I wake up feeling cold dead flesh against my skin. I know it's him, his body. Perhaps I am responsible, as the villagers say."

"Never." He kissed her hand and drew her close.

"Terrible as it probably was, I do wish I could remember, if only for an instant. Perhaps then King would leave me in peace."

"Where's Dr. Bickford now?"

"Died two years after King."

"And Sally?"

"Moved to Florida with her sister. But, it's no use. She will never say, and I won't ask after so many years. Ned, I'm sorry I blew up at you."

"Hush, my darling. Let's not start that again, it's me who should apologize."

"No, it isn't. I don't blame you, just as I don't blame the villagers for their suspicions, but there's a part of me that gets so angry at people. The newspapers at that time were so cruel, so quick to pass on any wild bit of information. Unfortunately, most of it was about me, and always bad."

She forced a smile, but Ned could see the tears threatening.

"Hey, what do you say we figure out what has to be done around here, do it, then take off the rest of the day off? Maybe have a picnic supper? It's going to be a pretty night. We could take a walk and then eat back near the old camp?"

Addie blinked back tears as she rose and pulled him to his feet. "I love you, Ned Fielding. Come on."

In late fall, the farm's work slowed considerably, but there were still orders to fill and harvesting of herbs and vegetables that couldn't wait. Addie took the garden duty and Ned saw to the delivery of the baskets. He had to do the errands he had neglected the day before. He also needed to call home, to make arrangements for the following week.

Martin had set the court date, for the settlement and final division of property for November 8th, a week from the coming Friday. Only ten days away.

Addie knew he was spending Thanksgiving with his children, but beyond that, he hadn't discussed his plans with her. She never asked and Ned said nothing, not quite knowing himself what was ahead. He sensed that his marriage and his family were still touchy subjects and until the divorce was final, he didn't feel it was fair to make plans with Addie, yet.

During the summer when his departure had been months away, there had been no urgency about the future. They had simply enjoyed each day as it unfolded, neither one of them worried about the next. Now, as his departure drew nearer, they seemed to tiptoe around the subject, neither one daring to make the first move.

After making the deliveries and running a few errands, he put in a call to Phil, to let him know when he'd be back.

"Great news, buddy. Marge's dying to see you. Me, too. Want us to get the guest room ready?"

"Thanks Phil, but the kids have rented a house by the river…the old Peterson place. I wanted to put us all up at the inn for a week at Thanksgiving, with the wedding and all, but they insisted on the Peterson place…eight bedrooms, I hear. Probably get lost tryin' to find the bathroom! There are advantages to having wealthy children."

"I'll say. Want some house guests over there?"

"Have to check with Ned and Syd on that. Janie's family's comin' in for the wedding. I think they'll be staying a few days anyway."

"How long you gonna be there?"

"Until after the wedding. They've taken the house for all of November and December. Claim they're gonna use it, but I know they're thinkin' of poor old Dad with no place to go. Crazy kids. I've told them over and over that I'll only be around for a few weeks, but they pay no attention."

"What're your plans after that?"

"Can you keep a secret, Phil?"

"Haven't I kept your beautiful Mrs. Barlow hush hush? Do your kids know? Did Marge blab to Penny?"

"Okay, okay. My plans do concern Addie. I, well, when the divorce is final, I'm going to ask her to marry me, if she'll have me."

"You sure about this, buddy?"

"Very."

There was a long pause before Phil said, "Well, then congratulations. I'm happy for you, Ned."

"Hold on. It's a little early for congratulations since the other half of this plan knows nothing about it. I'll get back to you. And Phil, mum's the word. Please. I'll tell the kids when I see them."

"Say no more. See you next week then? Dinner, Friday night, with Marge and me? We'll celebrate, or something."

"Thanks, Phil. See you Friday."

Neither Sydney nor Ned and Janie answered, so Ned dialed Sam Mahoney's office. Summoned by the receptionist, Sam Mahoney's voice boomed into the phone. "Where the hell have you been?"

"Hi to you too, Sam!"

"Ned, Ned, Ned. What the fuck am I gonna do with you?" Jesus Christ, Penny's taking you to the cleaners and I only hear about it three weeks ago. What the fuck do you expect me to do?"

"Nothing Sam. Really. Martin's been handling the whole thing. I just thought I'd better have someone stand with me the day of the hearing."

"Fine time to call me in! Jesus, Ned. Martin's handling the whole thing. That's the biggest fucking understatement of the century! To think he was your good friend! Penny's walking away with everything from what I can tell. What the hell kind of settlement is that?"

"It's fine, Sam. That's the way I wanted it. What do I need with a house full of furniture I never liked anyway? For that matter, what do I need with a house?"

"That's not the point and you know it. There are financial considerations, big ones. Penny's loaded already. If she wants the fucking house, your parents' goddamn house, I remind you, in case its slipped your mind, she can damn well pony up! She can afford a nice fat settlement to you. Instead, you're letting her steal the shirt off your back. Jesus, Ned!"

"Sam, we've been friends a long time. Have you ever known me to care about any of that shit? Ned and Syd are well taken care of. That's all I care about. So please, just do what I asked in my letter. Stand with me on the eighth, okay?"

"I might still be able to get a fairer settlement, if you'd let me take a crack at them."

"Sam, please."

"Okay, okay, but I don't like it. Shit, we could have cleaned up."

"Bye, Sam."

Ned hung up the phone on his friend, smiling. He had known Sam since grade school. Sam was always ready to fight, at the slightest provocation. A dispute in a marble game, a push on the playing field, or as the underdog in a legal dispute. It wasn't that he needed the money. The Mahoneys were right up there with the Pardingtons in the cash-flow department, but he sure loved a good fight, and he had never liked Penny. Not this time Sam, thought Ned, smiling as he walked back to the boat. This time Penny wins and wins big.

There was a letter from Sydney waiting in his mailbox on the dock. Ripping it open, he sat on the dock to read it:

"Dear Dad,

Long time no see. I miss you. Can't wait to be together. Hope you can stay thewhole two months. It's been so long since we were all together and the wedding will make Thanksgiving kind of hectic. Did you hear about the party we're giving on the ninth for Ned and Janie? Ellen's helping me. You can make it, can't you? I know the daybefore will be tough, but we'll get through it. Ned and I are planning to be there.

The next weekend we're hoping for a visit from Aunt Ruth and maybe Jean and Dickie. They'll be so happy to see you. Anyway, it'll be great to have so much time. Found a place to live after December yet? Maybe you and I can gohouse hunting? I'd love to help set up your new abode. Till the 8th—I love you!

S."

Help set up my house, Ned thought, chuckling as he collected the provisions, heading up the path to the cottage. He would have to go back to the village first thing tomorrow and call Sydney. This two month business would have to be nipped in the bud before things got out of hand. Why hadn't he thought to tell them he would only be staying a short time? Now they had booked him into social engagements for at least three weeks! And they still knew nothing about Addie.

CHAPTER 43

"You're quiet tonight."

Addie passed him a basket of warm, cardamom rolls. Folding back the home-spun blue cloth, he selected a sweet bun and marveled, as always, at the ease with which Addie created such foods. An afterthought to their simple dinner of chicken cassoulet, it went perfectly with the rest of the meal.

"I'm enjoying your wonderful cooking too much to speak."

"Your turn tomorrow night."

"Poor us."

"Nonsense. You're a great cook. Much too modest about your talents."

He smiled, but said nothing. Something was definitely wrong. Ned was usually loquacious at dinner, eager to share his day and hear about hers. Tonight he sat in stony silence, politely refusing to be drawn into conversation. He had been like this since his return from the village and she wondered what was wrong. Had someone said something to upset him? Had he heard unpleasant news from home? Or had he, perhaps, made a decision about his future? A decision that did not include her? Fearful, she dared not press him lest the reason for his strange behavior break her heart.

They had taken a long walk before setting out their picnic, which was spread on a soft red blanket on the matted grassy area of Ned's old campsite. They had dropped off the food earlier and taken their walk along the north-south path.

Then, they wended their way to the beach and walked halfway around the island before returning to the campsite via a new trail winding up from the beach on the south point. The new path, cut by Tim, Barry and Jack during their stay, opened the southern most point of the island, which had previously been inaccessible. The trail head afforded an unrestricted southern view across to the mainland and to the west and a clear view of the three other barrier islands.

They had stood at the trail head for a long while, watching the sunset, Ned's arm circling her waist, his touch light and tentative. She had wanted to speak, to ask him what was troubling him, but was too frightened. Now they sat, still silent as darkness closed in around them and sorrow twined 'round her heart.

He was leaving soon, but he had not told her when. He had told her many times that he loved her, but they'd never discussed the future, never talked about life beyond his months on the island. Self-doubt crept into her thoughts. No matter how much Addie told herself she'd be better off alone, she didn't believe it. Addie didn't know how she would survive having known such love, only to lose it.

She thought she knew him, but perhaps she didn't. Maybe she had simply been a pleasant diversion during his stay on Winward? But that wasn't Ned, at least not the Ned she knew. Was he a different person off-island? Had King been right all along and she was nothing but a trollop?

"Addie?"

She looked up to meet his eyes. She wanted nothing more than to throw herself into his arms and plead with him to stay and never to leave her.

"Are you okay? You look upset."

"Fine." Determined not to cry, she took a deep breath and fought back the tears.

He reached for a small knapsack he had insisted on packing and carrying along at the last minute. He placed the unopened sack in front of him, hastily clearing the plates off the blanket and stacking them carelessly on the grass.

She rose, moving to collect the dishes. "I'll just take these to the stream and rinse them off."

"No, wait, my darling." He grabbed hold of her wrist and gently pulled her back down to sit beside him on the blanket. He smiled, a mischievous glint in his eye as he unfastened the bag and brandished a bottle of champagne and two of her fluted glasses, which he had carefully packed in dish towels.

Mouth agape, she watched as he uncorked the bottle and handed her a glass, filling it, then his own.

"What's the occasion?" Was this to be their good-bye toast?

"Addie, I have no right to ask you this. I'm still legally married and my life is in shambles. Call me a louse, but what I'm trying to say is, I cannot imagine living without you, my beautiful, precious darling."

He rose, knelt beside her on one knee and took her hand. "Will you marry me when the divorce becomes final? I know I have no right to ask. God, I have nothing and you deserve better. You deserve a husband who will take care of you, but I cannot imagine my life without you in it. I can't go on making a life for myself without you in it. "

Addie threw her arms around him, champagne splashing over the blanket and down his back. "Yes!"

"Are you sure?"

"Yes." She buried her face in the crook of his neck...her face wet with tears of relief and happiness.

They held each other for several minutes before he said, "I have to go soon. Next week."

"I expected you might."

"You could come with me?"

"You haven't told your children anything about me, have you?"

"No."

"Then, I think you should go alone. I'd rather wait to meet them. I might be a shock and I would never want to spoil the wedding, or take away from Ned and Janie's special moment."

"Perhaps you're right. After all the excitement, I'll come back for you. Three weeks will seem like an eternity without you, my beautiful darling."

"It will pass quickly, with your family and your friends."

"I'll come back as soon as I can, my love. Then, we'll make plans. Pack you up, maybe take a trip. Where would you like to be married?"

"Ned?" A cold shudder passed through her. "I can't leave the island."

"Fine, we'll get a justice of the peace to come out and marry us here. Right on this spot if you like."

"No, you don't understand. I mean, I can't leave Winward to live somewhere else."

"Addie, I can't make a living here. I have a little money, but Penny is taking practically everything in the divorce. I'll have to work. There's no way I can support myself, never mind two people on what I have in the bank."

"You're forgetting that I make my own living, the fishing, the garden. I have more than enough to get by. Together, we would do fine, perhaps even expand, and take on more customers. There's my painting. Don't look so shocked. I've never shown my paintings to you. It's my winter pastime. I don't like to sell them, but I have in lean years."

"Addie, I can't. Visits yes, summers maybe, but live full-time here?"

The pounding in her chest deafened his last words as tears blurred her vision. "Then, it's settled," she said, rising unsteadily to her feet. "Let's clean up these things and go back."

"Addie, wait."

Ned's knees were weak and the horror of their separation hit him full force as waves of loneliness and loss washed over him.

"Please, Ned, let's just go."

Powerless to take back the words that had caused the terrible rift, he stood silent and watched her throw the dirty dishes willy-nilly into the basket. He wasn't shocked or even surprised by her suggestion. He had considered the idea of living on Winward, but he was taken aback by her refusal to consider an alternative. He knew her love matched his, knew it without question. He also knew that she loved the island, but he had assumed that frequent visits would be enough. Aran was a problem, but the coyote was more than capable of taking care of herself. In fact, she hunted for most of her food as it was. If they came often enough, even every weekend, he had reasoned that Addie would be happy in town.

How shortsighted he had been. Addie would never be happy away from the sea, away from her gardens, away from a life filled with work that she loved. How could he have thought otherwise? The island was part of her. A move would destroy her. Winward represented a mirror image of the strong independent woman she had become, its craggy cliffs and heart wrenching beauty reflecting its lone inhabitant. King Barlow had nearly destroyed her, but she had survived and emerged from the depths of that destruction to forge a life of strength and purpose. How could he ask her to leave, yet how could he stay? The idea seemed preposterous.

CHAPTER 44

They'd talked very little that night, retiring early. In the morning, she rose and was gone by the time he came down. For several days they lived together, ate together, even slept in the same bed, but spoke little. With horror, Ned reflected on the similarities between this existence and his marriage.

Three days before he was due to depart, he sat her down after another silent dinner. "Addie, we need to talk."

"There's nothing more to say."

"Yes, there is. I understand your wish to remain on the island. I just can't make that kind of commitment until I've settled things at home…maybe after I go back, get the divorce behind me, and figure out what I'm doing. I can't live without you. If it means we must live here, we'll figure something out."

"It's settled, Ned." Her sad eyes belied her icy tone. "I would never want Winward to be a place of exile for you. You would grow to hate me for keeping you here. I couldn't stand that. I'd rather you go now."

"Addie, that's just not an option."

"Please, let's not talk about it. Can we just enjoy your last days?"

"I just want you to know that I haven't made my decision. What I'm asking is, am I too late? Can I come back if I want?"

Ned drew her near, arms enclosing her, and Addie returned his embrace.

"Always."

Those last days, their lovemaking became a frenzied holding on, bodies crashing together in desperate longing. Each night grew wilder with their rough passion, leaving them exhausted. They sleepwalked through daily routines. Ned packed while Addie worked the farm.

The last night had been almost brutal with Ned ravishing her on the living room floor after dinner. He then carried her up to bed and apologized, but she wanted him again and again, until they both lay spent and sore on damp sheets. 'What's happened to us?' he thought, holding her trembling body against him.

The nightmare came just before dawn, and Ned held her tight, wondering how he could leave her to face the terrors alone.

In the morning, they stood together on the dock, a beautiful day unfolding before them.

Addie kissed him for the hundredth time. "I'll be fine."

"I'll write. I'll send a phone number and a time to call. Will you call?"

"Yes."

"I love you."

"And, I, you. Now go, before I cry. Please, I don't want to you to remember me with tears in my eyes."

Ned hopped into the canoe, started the motor and pushed off. "I'll be back soon."

She stood watching until the canoe rounded the point, and then turned to give in to her tears. As she reached the cliffs, the canoe was just visible, a tiny red sliver in the steel blue of the channel, and she whispered a silent good-bye, telling herself that he would never return.

CHAPTER 45

"So, how was it?"

Ned sat at the dinner table. His dear friends, Marge and Phil Bodington stared at him, waiting to hear how the afternoon had gone. His memory of the hearing was already a blur. Three hours earlier, he had sat at Sam Mahoney's side as the judge declared his marriage of twenty-two years legally dead. When it was over, Penny swished by him, resplendent in scarlet and black. Those colors had always suited her sharp, angular features. Ned noticed her hand draped possessively over her attorney's arm and said a silent prayer for Martin. Did he have any idea what he was getting into?

Ned had smiled at his now-ex-wife, giving her a thumbs up and Penny's face fell, an angry mask replacing the smugness of a second earlier. He was supposed to be heartbroken, or at least broken, defeated and humiliated. Instead he seemed to be mocking her with his ridiculous grin.

"Good luck, Pen," he said, turning away from her icy glare.

Martin tried to follow him to say something, but she quickly seized control of him.

"Martin, don't you dare speak to him."

Ned hastened down the steps of the granite courthouse and broke into a run as he hit the sidewalk of Main Street.

Greenleaf, true to its name, had streets lined with trees. Elm, maple, oak and beech trees, planted hundreds of years ago by the founding fathers, created a gorgeous canopy that shaded the residents in the summer and rewarded them with a riot of color in autumn. The fall's canopy…brilliant oranges, fiery reds and muted yellows, tinged with remnants of summer's green, turned the village into a flaming, sunlit paradise for "leaf peepers," tourists who invaded the peaceful village every fall. By November, the foliage display had fallen to the ground and been raked away and forgotten. Then the smaller evergreens, interspersed between the deciduous giants, took center stage, upstaging the naked skeletons all around them. The tiny pines and firs, their berries bright, their greens, pale lime to deep forest hues, shone stark and lively against the white clapboard storefronts lining Main Street.

Today, Ned hardly noticed the trees or stores as he ran to his car, to make his escape. He had insisted upon driving alone, urging Ned and Sydney to stay with their mother. He had been thankful at his foresight and his children's compliance as he sped away from the courthouse.

Suddenly, realizing his friends had been staring at him for several minutes, he shrugged and grinned. "Not too bad."

"And?" Phil asked, eying him.

"It's a weird feeling, you know? I had this urge to go straight to Adlers' Hardware to buy cans of paint, to paint all the walls of my home a new color, but then I remembered, I don't have a home to paint."

Marge nodded. "You want a fresh start. That's understandable."

"How'd you make out, anyway, buddy?"

"Fine. Well actually I got nothing, except my own personal accounts and my books and papers. She let me have the furniture from the den. Thought she might give in and let old Haggardy come with me, but apparently not. I'll miss the old guy."

"Mahoney couldn't do any better than that for you? With all Penny's money and it being your house? Christ, Ned, you should have gotten a decent lawyer!"

"Phil, we've been through this before. I want it this way."

"Course you do," Marge said, patting his hand and giving her husband a look. "Let's talk about something else. I want to hear about your lady friend, the mysterious Mrs. Barlow. Phil certainly was taken with her, weren't you dear? Couldn't talk about anything else for days after he got back."

Ned looked at his friend curiously, "Oh?"

"Well, you have to admit, she's unusual. And I knew you were smitten. Fact is, I like her. I think Marge would too."

"That's why I'm asking. When do I get to meet her? Why didn't you bring her along?"

"She would have come, but thought it best to wait. I haven't told the kids about her yet. I decided to break the news first."

"What news? Are you two getting…?"

"Married? I don't know Marge." Turning to Phil, he added, "She won't leave the island."

"You mean right now?"

"Never."

Phil whistled, scratching his chin. "Uh, oh, trouble in paradise."

"I bet she'll change her mind," Marge piped in. "What could you possible do on that tiny island? How would you live? How does she live?"

"She makes a good living from her gardens and the fishing."

"That's fine for her, but what about you? Your work and your research? How could you give it all up for some godforsaken island? Did you know about this, Phil?"

"Now calm down, Margie. Ned hasn't said he's going, have you buddy? Besides, I can think of worse places to live."

Tired of the discussion, Ned longed to go home to bed, "Truthfully, guys, I don't know what I want. I'm gonna to use the next few weeks to think about it. I can't live without her, though, that's for certain."

Driving home, he thought about Addie and wanted desperately to hear her voice. When he arrived at the rented Peterson house, mansion really, he sat down to write her an e-mail:

"My dearest Addie,

The hearing went well. I am now a free man. Free to marry you my love, whenever you say the word. I'm now ensconced in the Peterson mansion at the edge of town. It's a huge brick and ivy affair, white columns in front, six car garage around to the rear. I feel a little silly knockin' around this big ol' place by myself, but the kids'll be here soon…

Gardens here must be beautiful in the summer. Nothing like yours, of course—too stuffy and formal, but there are acres and acres of them. Rose gardens, topiary, fountains, reflecting pools, rock gardens. You name it, it's probably out there. God, I miss you, my darling.

Had dinner with Phil and Marge tonight. You'd like Marge. I hope you two will meet soon. Phil sends his regards. Dinner party tomorrow night with old friends, but other than that, I'll spend a quiet weekend.

Will spend most of next week at SENCA, going over everything with Phil. I guessI have to do some interviews, journals and so forth—my least favorite occupation.

You have my cell number. Please call, if you can. I miss you, sweetheart. Did Isay that already? Sending all my love and a kiss to you, my darling, my love, my life.

N."

After hitting "send," he closed his laptop and got ready for bed. The strain of the day overtook him and he collapsed onto the bed, asleep instantly. When he woke the next morning, he sat up, disoriented, expecting to find himself in their bedroom at the cottage. An aching loneliness tugged at his heart.

He gazed around at the small room at the end of the corridor that he had selected for himself. It was furnished with a ladder back chair, a small dresser and narrow bed with a Navajo patterned bedspread. He had chosen this room, knowing it would not appeal to the others. Very small, it had no adjoining bathroom. He knew also that they'd get after him for choosing it when there were five or six grander rooms available, but he liked it. Its sparse furnishings and modest dimensions made him feel comfortable and secure, unlike how he knew he would feel in any of the larger rooms with their huge canopy beds, fireplaces and Empire armoires.

Only a few weeks, he told himself. He dressed in old clothes for a morning walk. Better get it in now, he thought, before the hordes arrive.

CHAPTER 46

Sydney arrived first, followed several hours later by her brother and Janie. From the moment his children arrived, Ned was caught up in a whirlwind of social engagements interspersed with his SENCA work. He spent nearly every day at the office, cataloguing specimens, transcribing and organizing his notes and working with the cartographer to revise, redraw, and rework the island's map.

From the time he arrived home each afternoon, his kids had his every minute planned. Outings and dinners stretched into the wee hours of the morning. He didn't mind; he loved his children and enjoyed their company, but he had not had a moment to think and decide what he would do, or where he would go after Thanksgiving.

He told the kids that he would be leaving the Sunday after Thanksgiving. The wedding was to be Friday, after which Ned and Janie planned a short honeymoon on Nevis, an island in the West Indies. Ned had already been assigned to airport shuttle duty Saturday morning after the wedding. Then his duties would be over. That would leave the afternoon and evening to pack up. Where was he going? This question, which Ned asked himself with regularity, was echoed again and again in his children's queries about his somewhat nebulous plans for the future.

"Stay here, in the house, Dad. We rented it for you, so you could have some time to figure things out."

"I know Syd, and I do appreciate it."

Ned smiled at his daughter, no longer a child, she'd grown into a beautiful young woman, independent and strong-willed, full of all the compassion and warmth that her mother lacked. She had Penny's delicate features, the high cheekbones and the straight, almost perfect nose, and her mother's slender frame, but she had Ned's coloring. Her hair, while straight like her mother's, was sandy, and her eyes were the same hazel green as her father's, the same twinkle as Ned's when she smiled.

Ned Jr. reached across the table to grasp Janie's hand. "Then, stay Dad. The house is yours. Janie and I will be in and out the whole time. Hey, when will we ever live in something this size, again? It'd be great to spend time together."

How lucky you are, Ned thought, watching his son gaze affectionately at his fiancée. Janie, freckle-faced and rosy cheeked, looked the picture of happiness and good health. Penny had been at her most beautiful in pregnancy, all her angles softened, her demeanor calmer, more relaxed.

Ned smiled, regarding the three of them before he spoke. "There's a part of me that would like nothing better than to stay here with you guys. You know that, but I can't live off my kids. Not yet anyway. And I've, well, I've met someone."

Sydney sat up, hands gripping the table. "Who?"

"I've asked her to marry me."

"What? Where?" Mouth agape, his daughter stared at him as if he sprouted horns. "When? You mean, that's why you and mom split up?"

"Come off it Syd, you know Dad. He wouldn't have had an affair, would you Dad?"

Laughing, Ned replied, "No, I wouldn't. Least I don't think I would. No, this relationship is new. It's happened very recently, the past few months actually."

"On the island?"

"Yup."

"But, who? I thought it was a wildlife refuge, that you were the only one out there?"

"Almost Syd, but not quite. SENCA owns half of Winward Island. The other half is owned by a woman, Adelaide Barlow. It was left to her many years ago by her husband."

"How old is she then?" Janie asked, eyes wide as saucers.

Janie was already like a daughter to him, Ned reflected and he smiled, squeezing her hand. "Younger than me, but, to be perfectly honest, I don't know. Let's see, she was married at eighteen, marriage lasted nearly five years 'till her husband died, and she's been alone for about twelve years. That makes her—"

"Thirty-five," Sydney said, her voice hard.

"About that, I'd guess."

"So Dad, when are we gonna meet her? Why didn't you bring her back with you? To the wedding," Ned asked. "Janie and I would have been happy to have her."

"I know, son, but I…we thought it best to hold off, for your sake and your mom's. I honestly don't know what the heck I'm doin' and where I'm going."

"I wouldn't worry too much about Mom," Sydney said. "She's been all over town with Martin Lawson. Serves her right."

"I don't want to serve her right, Syd, and neither do you. Your Mother's been through enough."

"How can you talk that way, Dad? She has given you the royal screw! God, you let her take everything! Everything! She now has anything that was of any value that belonged to the two of you, even your own house. She's such an incredible bitch, it's beyond belief. You just let her walk all over you!"

"Shut up, Syd. It's Dad's business." His son's gaze was sad as he regarded his father and sister.

Ned took his daughter's hand. "Darling, listen to me. I didn't want any of it. I don't know what I can say to convince you of that. The house and all the things in it were hers. Your mother's, not mine. I don't have a use for them and never really liked them. They mean a great deal to your mom. They mean nothing to me. Yes, the house was important to me when you were growing up, but now that you're launched, I'm happy for her to have it. It's her home as much as mine."

"But, the money, you could have gotten a settlement. That's what people do. They don't just walk away and say 'have it all.' Hasn't Sam Mahoney ever heard of division of property?" Sydney's voice was less shrill and the storm was passing. Penny had never gotten along with her daughter and the divorce had widened their rift.

"I have some money put aside. Penny couldn't touch my own investments, darling. She took the house, and you're right, it was our biggest asset, but she left my own capital alone. It was fair. Your mother put her life's blood into that house. It was her house."

"No it wasn't. It was Gramps' and Nana's. Your house."

"That was a long time ago, sweetheart. I believe, in the end, Gramps and Nana would have agreed with me. The house belonged to your mother."

Sydney scowled, the fight gone. "Doubt it."

"Where are you gonna live?" Janie's voice filled the silence.

"That's an issue. Addie, doesn't want to leave the island. Or, should I stay, won't leave the island. And, I'm not sure whether I can live there full-time."

"What would you do on the island?" his son asked. "Is there anything on the mainland, nearby? I don't know that area too well. It's not far from UMass Dartmouth, is it?"

"Forty-five minutes," Ned replied. "But, I'm not sure I'm interested in a return to academia, at least not right now, son."

"Then what?"

"That's the big question."

Ned regarded the three and decided they had now switched roles. He had become the child and they the parents. Here they were, grilling him on what he was going to do with his life. "I'll keep you posted."

"We'll help you out, Dad. If you need a loan or something?"

"See what I mean?" Sydney interrupted. "If he'd gotten a decent settlement, he wouldn't need a loan."

She has more of her mother in her than she knows, Ned thought wistfully. "Now hold on a second. I just finished telling you, your dear old Dad is fine. I may not be as flush as you three, but I've got enough to get by. And, I'm about to collect a nice paycheck for the last six months, when I've been living rent-free, I might remind you."

"And you still get royalties on your books, don't you Ned?" Janie asked, referring to three volumes of essays he'd published over the years, expository pieces dealing with biology and evolution. They'd been written in layman's language and had attracted a healthy following over the years. All three were still in print, in paperback.

"Thank you, Janie. As a matter of fact, I do."

"Humph," Sydney said, rounding the table to hug him. "Let's go play a vicious game of bridge and forget about all this. But, Dad, remember, we still want to meet this younger woman soon, don't we guys?"

CHAPTER 47

While Ned's time flew in a spiraling whirlwind of activities, Addie's slowed to a standstill. Loneliness dragged at her heels each day and she went through her daily routines in a kind of suspended slow motion. Ordinarily, she savored the quieter days of late fall when the weather turned cool and the harvest was in. She screwed storm windows into place and stored screens in the barn. She cleaned up the gardens and stacked lobster pots along the barn's south wall, then mulched the remaining crops with hay. The thick hay blanket kept the greens and root vegetables warm for a few more weeks until the ground froze completely.

The fields, tawny in their fall coats, fell silent as birds departed for warmer climes and woodland creatures…woodchucks, foxes, field mice, moles, rabbits and raccoon went underground. With the animals' disappearance, hunting became a challenge for Aran and she spent most of her daylight hours in search of game, which grew scarcer and scarcer.

In November, she pressed apples for cider and made apple and peach butters, which she sold in the village. Her orchard was small, but like her other harvests, its yield bountiful. Her cider was prized above all others.

Since her early days on the island, Addie had donated one basket of food each week to St. Timothy's, the tiny Presbyterian Church sitting at the edge of the village. The Reverend Chase had provided solace and comfort at the time of her husband's death.

Aside from Jim Talbot, her lawyer, Al Chase had been the only person to stand behind her, the only person who believed in her. "Don't shut yourself away, Adelaide," the good man had begged, upon hearing her plans to settle on the island. "People's talk will die down and with God's help and your strength, you'll come through this."

While she had not taken the minister's advice, Addie never forgot his kindness. Hence the baskets, taken by Mr. Chase himself every Tuesday to the children's home in Derryville, and the cases of cider donated to the church's harvest fair, which was held on the second Saturday in November.

When she dropped off the cider, Al Chase caught up with her. "Join us this year, won't you, my dear?"

"Thank you, Reverend, but I have so much to do."

"Please, Adelaide, a few hours can't hurt."

"Perhaps."

Addie waved as she drove off, the battered green truck kicking up dust. She looks different, he thought, watching her go. It had been months since he had last seen Adelaide Barlow, but there had been a change. A change for the better, he thought with pleasure. The sadness is there, but her burden has lessened. He wondered absently if the change had anything to do with the stranger, the scientist, who'd been living out on the island. He hoped so.

Addie received Ned's e-mails, sometimes two or three a day and always replied immediately, with fingers crossed that the unreliable Internet service would cooperate. After a day spent indoors, she wrote:

"Dearest Ned,

The first snow has fallen on Winward. Aran has spent the morning playing in it and I have come inside to sit by the fire and be lazy. I read a little, snoozed a little, ate a little. Very lazy! A kind of torpor has come over me, a listlessness that I can't seem to shake. Perhaps writing to you will wake me up. Seeing you would be even better!

Things are quiet now. Branwen has departed, Gwydyon will follow soon. The work of shutting up the farm is nearly completed and I am making the transition towinter. It's very hard. I don't want to let go of this summer and all it has meant to me.Soon, the paints and my easel will come out and I'll be fully immersed in winter projects.

How are you holding up with all your activities? Your schedule sounds much more grueling than mine. Not a minute passes that my thoughts are not of you. Take care, my love.

A.

P.S. I will try to phone again Wednesday, mid-day."

Ned had missed her two previous phone calls and she desperately wanted to hear his voice. Unprepared for the depths of loneliness she'd experienced the past weeks, she was shocked by the desolation she had felt since his departure.

After King's death, she had been lonely, but nothing like this. Although relieved to be free of her husband's abuse and brutality, she had felt so empty and friendless during that period as she struggled to survive each day. She had not loved King, but now that she had experienced love and the comfort and warmth of its embrace, she no longer felt complete without Ned. Some of the fierce self-sufficiency that had sustained her over the past twelve years had been chipped away by love and the connection to another human being. His leaving had thus left her feeling bereft and rudderless. She knew she could take care of herself, make her living, and survive, but that was no longer enough. Without Ned, there was a bone-numbing loneliness that no amount of work could fill.

By the week of Thanksgiving, she had resolved to leave the island if she must. Ned had mentioned nothing about his plans in his letters. Instead they were filled with stories about his children and expressions of love for her. She knew he wouldn't press her. That was Ned, always putting her feelings above his own. It would be up to her to make the decision, up to her to say she would go. Ned would never ask again, of this she was certain.

Cell phone service on the island was so spotty, that she had made arrangements to call Ned from the Rudders' land line. In fact, in the three weeks since Ned's departure, Addie had made contacts that had been unthinkable during her previous twelve years. She had actually visited Elsie's and ordered a cup of tea, to go, but she had stepped in, even chatted briefly with Elsie. On another occasion, she had stopped for a fairly lengthy chat with Abe Rudder, and for brief intervals two other days.

The first conversation had been at her initiation. She had cornered him as he closed up one noon, less than a week after Ned's departure.

"Mr. Rudder, could I speak with you?"

Shocked, but trying to hide it, he said, "Talk away."

"Could we step inside, please?"

"Guess so."

When they had settled, Abe into his rickety oak swivel chair, she onto a filthy canvas deck chair, she began, "Mr. Rudder, Abe, I, well, I'd like to pay for the use of your phone. I'll be making some calls."

"To Fielding, no doubt."

Drawing a breath, she continued, ignoring the interruption. "My cell service on the island, as here in the village, is unreliable. I need to make some calls. Long distance. I'd rather make them here than at the post office. Could I perhaps give you some money, or note down the numbers and settle up when you get the bill?"

"Where's he gone, anyway? Back to Greenfield or wherever he's from?"

"Please Abe. What do you say? Can I use the phone or not?"

"'Spect it'd be all right. Just jot the numbers in my notebook here. Now, are you gonna answer my question or not?"

"Yes, Ned, Mr. Fielding, has gone back to Greenleaf."

"Comin' back?"

"I don't know."

"You'd like him to, wouldn't ya?"

Tempted to rise, leaving the nosy old man and his precious telephone, she forced herself to answer calmly, "Yes, I would."

This seemed to disarm him. To her surprise, he said, "Me too."

From then on, they had been, if not bosom buddies, at least civil to one another, and the arrangement with the phone had provided several more opportunities to become reacquainted with one another.

CHAPTER 48

It was mid-morning, the Wednesday before Thanksgiving, when she docked alongside the boat house. The *Pickle Shack,* boarded up in the cold weather, was surrounded by boats pulled out of the water for the winter. Abe still spent his mornings at the office, but took a two-hour lunch break at Elsie's before heading home for the day. She knew if she caught him on his way to lunch, he'd leave her alone with the phone with the admonition to shut up the office behind her.

When she arrived, she found Abe on the phone, engaged in a heated argument. Waving, she stepped back outside. The village had had more snow than Winward, and the streets were lined with grey-black walls of plowed snow. Icicles hung from the overhanging roofs of the store fronts and the harbor was scattered with chunks of ice and miniature glaciers dotted the beach. A lone gull circled the sky and dipped its wings to catch the faint rays of sun, its white form disappearing against the grey of the western sky, then reappearing against the inky backdrop of the winter sea.

"Come on in, Mrs. B. I'm headed for lunch, so the phone's all yours. I expect you're tryin' to reach Fielding?"

She nodded.

"Good luck. If you get him, say hello for me and Rufus. That was him on the phone. Been at that school less than two months and he wants to quit, stupid kid."

"Why?"

"Can't hack English class. Always was a poor reader. The boy never seemed to catch on in the early grades. After that it was too late. Don't know why the heck he needs English in a vocational school anyway. Got some big paper due next week—scared to death. Comin' home for the holiday tonight. Doesn't want to go back. Wants to tell 'em today."

"That's a shame."

"Well, he ain't. I told him no way. He's paid up through January and he's stickin' it out 'till then and that's that!"

"Abe, do you think he'd let me help him? With the English, I mean? If he were to bring his books out to the cottage, or maybe we could work together in the library this weekend?"

"I don't know, Mrs. B. Why would you want to help us? After all the years I've been such a horse's behind?"

"I could have tried to make friends before."

"Not with old fools like me around. We were idiots. He, yer husband played us like he was the damned pied piper. All his money, the easy life he gave so many of us. When he messed up, we just up and looked the other way, refusing to see what the bastard was doing."

"Abe, don't. Please. It was a long time ago, and I'd rather let go of the past, if you don't mind. Please tell Rufus to let me know if he needs help. I'll stop in to check about it on Friday. If I knew what books he was reading, it would help. I'll leave my cell number here and you can leave a message, even if I don't pick up. Now, aren't you going to be late for lunch?"

"'Spect so." He threw on his coat. "Thanks for the offer. I'll tell Rufus."

The door rattled shut, leaving Addie alone in the stuffy office, the phone already in her hand.

Ned answered on the first ring.

"Ned?" She knew it was him, but wanted to hear his voice speaking to her, wanting him never to stop.

"Addie, thank God. My darling, how are you?" Then, when she didn't respond, "This is Addie, isn't it?"

"Yes, I'm fine."

"Where are you? I'm sorry I missed your other calls. Every time there was a crisis. Are you at home? Is this a good connection?"

"It's fine, I'm fine. I'm calling from Abe Rudder's office. My cell service is unreliable, even in the village."

"You're kidding! How'd that happen?"

"Believe it or not, Abe and I have become friends of a sort. Well, perhaps, friends is too strong a word, but we're at least civil. It's wonderful to hear your voice. How are you?"

"Fine. No, terrible. I miss you desperately."

"Me, too. Ned, I have something I want to say to you before we say anything else. I've done a great deal of thinking since you left. I love Winward, you know that, perhaps too much, but I do. But, well, I will leave with you, to go where you need to go. If we can visit, perhaps live close enough to visit often?"

Ned sat in stunned silence, moved to tears by her words and the effort it had obviously cost her to utter them, and the great sacrifice she willing to make for him. "Addie, I can't ask you to leave Winward."

"I want to. I want to be with you, and, well, it might be good for me to get out in the world again. You never know, we'll see."

"I don't know what to say."

"Say nothing, just hurry back, and we'll plan and decide when you get here. Unless you've changed your mind about us?"

"Are you kidding? Never. What about Aran?"

There was a long pause before she said, softly, "Aran can take care of herself." He listened, her voice thick, choked up. She was crying.

"Addie."

"It's just that I miss you so much. Ned, please hurry back."

Although he did not doubt that she missed him, he also knew that that was not the reason for her tears. Not wishing to upset her further, he dropped the subject.

"What has been happening down there, besides your budding romance with Abe Rudder?"

She laughed and told him about her days. Ned sat back, loving the sound of her voice.

"Oh," she said, at one point. "I had a note from Jim Talbot last week. Remember, my lawyer? An announcement, actually. He's just gotten married and he wrote a short message on the back of the announcement. He and his wife, Carol live in Swansea. Isn't that quite close to Greenleaf?"

"'Bout half an hour. That's where he's practicing?"

"I assume so. He didn't say. Anyway, it was nice to hear from him. You'd like him."

Ned longed to hold her. He felt empty and anxious without her, "I love you, my darling. Just as soon as the wedding is over and the kids are off, I'll be back. I wish you could come here."

"Soon, my darling, I want to meet Ned and Sydney and Janie, but we'll have time soon. Listen, I have to go. Abe's being very generous, but I don't way to overstay my welcome."

"Are you sure you're okay?"

"Fine, but I should go."

"All right, but call again, if you can. I'll be here all day tomorrow."

"I won't leave the island tomorrow. Friday I may be occupied, helping Rufus with his school work."

He opened his mouth to ask, but then though better of it. Nothing this woman did would ever cease to amaze him. "I'll try and get going early Sunday. I should be to Tripp's Landing by four. I had to return SENCA's canoe, but I'll call ahead and hire someone to bring me out."

"I can come over and meet you."

"No, darling. I don't want to keep you waiting. Besides, I want you all to myself when we meet, not stuck in the middle of a bunch of gawking villagers."

"Well, I'm happy to come, if you change your mind."

"I'll get out there. Don't worry…even if I have to swim, I'll be there."

"Bye, my love."

"Three days," he whispered, as she gently returned the antique receiver to its cradle.

"Three days." she echoed as she wiped tears from her cheeks. Three days and perhaps she'd have to leave Winward and Aran forever. So be it, she thought, closing the office door behind her.

CHAPTER 49

"What a sweetie she is," Margie Bodington said, as she, Phil, and Ned watched Janie and Ned Jr. dance their first dance as husband and wife.

"I'll say." Phil nodded. "They met at Colgate, didn't they?"

Ned grinned. "They were roommates the last two years, but, don't tell the Nickersons."

Sally and Bob Nickerson, Janie's parents, mortified by her condition, had been greatly relieved at the couple's decision to have a small wedding. Aside from a handful of friends, mostly college buddies, the wedding had been just family. Ned had insisted on having Phil and Marge. "They're family anyway," Sydney had proclaimed. Penny brought Martin Lawson.

Throughout their college years, Janie and Ned had spent most holidays and weekends with Ned's parents, preferring their more casual attitudes concerning premarital sex to the Nickerson's rather prudish insistence on them sleeping in separate bedrooms. Penny, for all her social airs and convictions, took a liberal minded view of premarital sex. She could hardly do otherwise, given her own history. While stiff and formal at present, Penny had opened her home willingly to her children and their friends during their growing up years.

Ned's attitude had always been the more the merrier. He happily left them to their own devices and joined them for many a communal dinner. Margaret, the cook, was always a little frazzled by the end of the school vacations with her domain invaded by "so many moderns."

While they did not approve of Janie's condition, the Nickersons liked Ned. They approved of the union—not because of the Pardington fortune, but because they genuinely cared about their daughter's happiness. Ned Fielding Jr. clearly made her happy.

Ned was glad his friends were with him. Marge, resplendent in bright green chiffon, the dress tight across her hips and ample bosom, had chatted nonstop since their arrival from the church. Phil, arm draped across his wife's round, plump shoulders, looked shabbily dapper in a Harris Tweed sport coat and gray flannels. Both men wore SENCA ties, the agency logo in bright reds and yellows across the green silk background.

"Oh Dad," Sydney had exclaimed that morning noticing the tie. "Don't you have anything snazzier?"

"Perhaps we should invite Janie's parents to sit with us?" Marge whispered, "They look a little forlorn."

Before Ned had time to reply, his daughter swished by and grabbed his arm. "Warning, Mom has arrived, Martin in tow. She knows about Addie and she's pissed."

"How?"

"Ned blabbed the news when they were out to dinner with Mom and Martin last night. Guess she went a little crazy. Thought you oughta be forewarned!" Sydney flew off, joining a group of friends.

Ned watched his daughter saunter off to join her friends and smiled to himself. Despite her disdain for her mother, the two women dressed alike and moved alike. Truth be told, they looked more like sisters than mother and daughter. How furious Sydney would be if he pointed out the similarities, but they were there.

"What's up, buddy? Anything wrong?"

"Nothing Phil. Just don't get too close to me when Penny's around. You might get kicked."

"What?" Marge craned to hear the men.

"She's apparently been informed about Addie, and she's none too happy."

Phil's eyes scanned the room. "What business is it of hers?"

"None, but have you ever known that to stop Pen? She has her own ideas about what is and is not her business. I think you're right. Let's ask the Nickersons to join us. I'll be right back."

Halfway across the room, she intercepted him. "Well, you certainly didn't waste any time!"

"Hello, Penny, Martin." Ned nodded at the man beside her. Impeccably dressed in a navy wool suit, his hair was thinning with a hint of grey sprinkled through the slick, dark mane.

Lawson smiled and extended his hand. "Ned, we hear that congratulations may soon be in order for you. And, of course, congratulations today, as father of the groom."

"Thanks, Martin. Good to see you. How have you been?"

Before the other man could reply, Penny grabbed hold of Ned's arm. "Would you excuse us a minute, Martin dear? We won't be long." Not waiting for Martin's reply, she propelled Ned towards the door. "I need to speak with you, outside."

"Fine." Ned opened the door and ushered her into the lobby. "Let's go to the taproom."

"I prefer the lounge."

"Okay, lead the way."

After the waitress had retreated to fetch them each a glass of wine, she turned on him. "Just what do you think you're doing?"

"My dear, I don't have the vaguest idea what you are talking about."

"You most certainly do! You couldn't wait, could you? You had to humiliate me…even at the end!"

"What are you talking about?"

"I'm talking about this woman. This mysterious person you've been carrying on with. Is she the reason you took the job? How long has this been going on?"

"Penny, I can see that you're upset, but this is none of your business. I can't do this anymore. I'm sorry the kids' mention of Addie has upset you. I wouldn't have willingly upset you for all the world, especially not on Ned and Janie's day."

"Addie, so that's her name! None of my business? My husband having an affair is none of my business!"

"Penny, stop it now! I'm not your husband anymore, remember? Besides, you've been seeing Martin for months."

"Is that what you think? That Martin and I? How stupid can you be? Martin is my lawyer. He's been giving me legal advice, for which I've paid him handsomely, I might add."

"Come off it, Penny. You and Martin were going to Aruba together. If it hadn't been for the wedding, you two would have been on the beach right now. Are you honestly going to tell me the trip had to do with your legal affairs?"

"That's a lie. I was taking that trip alone and anyone who says otherwise is misinformed."

"Penny, can we please stop this? This is Janie and Ned's day. Let's not spoil it by fighting. We're divorced. Let's accept it and move on. And, just to set the record straight, I met Addie in May. I had no idea that she existed when I took the job."

"Just tell me what she has that I don't. A barefooted, country bumpkin, living on some God forsaken island. What could you possible see in a person like that? Is it a Robinson Crusoe type thing?"

"That's enough."

"No, it isn't. I have to know. What is the appeal of this woman? What did I do wrong?"

"Penny, we've been through this a thousand times. It's nothing you did. It's me. Oh Christ, why am I even bothering?"

"Oh, poor, pitiful Penny. Is that it? Poor Penny who just can't get it together. Well, I loved you, Ned. I still love you, though God knows why. If you'd just come back, we could try again. The house isn't the same without you."

"Penny, please, don't. We're divorced. You're gonna be fine. I can't be there for you anymore. I haven't been there for you for years. Open your eyes. Martin adores you. He worships the ground you walk on. Give him a chance and maybe you'll find the happiness I could never give you."

Her shoulders sagged, conceding defeat. "That's it then, isn't it?"

"Yes."

"Where will you go? What will you do?

"Honestly, I'm not sure."

"The same Ned." She gave him a rueful smile. "Well, good luck. To you, and to your island mistress."

"Thanks."

As they stepped back into the ballroom to join the others, Penny turned to glance back at him over her shoulder. "And, of course, now you understand why I had to take it all?"

"Yup." He reached out and squeezed her hand. "I know you'll enjoy it."

The rest of the reception was a blur of dancing, eating and drinking. Too much drinking Ned decided the following morning when he awoke with a pounding headache. Janie looked radiant as they danced together, her swelling belly draped modestly in a simple muslin gown.

Janie looked up, smiling at her new father-in-law. "She makes you happy, doesn't she?"

"Who?" Ned asked, absently, still thinking about Penny.

"Your Addie. You're almost starry-eyed when you talk about her."

He kissed Janie's cheek. "Yes, I guess I am, sweetheart. She makes me very happy and, my darling daughter, so do you."

Janie nuzzled against him, her eyes wet with tears. "Thank you, Dad."

Ned pulled out his handkerchief, drying her tears. "Hey, this is a wedding. People are supposed to be happy!"

"I am happy. I love you, Ned, and your son, too."

"Ned's a lucky man."

"And, we both want to meet her, real soon."

"This can be done."

With that, Ned whirled her back to her husband and escorted Marge to the dance floor.

CHAPTER 50

After dropping the honeymooners at the airport with promises to write and call soon, Ned headed east on the highway, towards Swansea, instead of taking the Post Road back to Greenleaf. Wednesday, after talking to Addie, he had called Jim Talbot and asked to see him. They had arranged to meet at the latter's office at noon on Saturday.

Ned wasn't sure why he was going, but the need to learn the truth about King Barlow's death still nagged at him. He suspected that Jim Talbot knew less than Addie about the events of that terrible night, but he had to ask. He hadn't told Addie of his plan as he didn't want to worry her and upset their reunion.

When he arrived at the one-story, glass-fronted office building, Jim Talbot was waiting in the lobby. He looked not a day older than his newspaper photos of twelve years ago. He stepped forward and shook Ned's hand, then ushered him back to his office, a small cubicle, in the honeycombed infrastructure of *Taylor, Lane and Brownell.*

Ned noticed the other's hair was sparse on top, revealing a bald patch beneath a few thin strands of hair, but the babyish face hadn't a wrinkle on it. Talbot wore a sports jacket over a navy pullover sweater, no tie and blue jeans, slightly worn, but neatly pressed.

"So, Mr. Fielding, you know Addie, Mrs. Barlow, I mean. How is she?"

"She's fine. And, please, call me Ned. She speaks very highly of you, Mr. Talbot."

"Jim." The man smiled, eying Ned with a curious expression. "How can I help you?"

"I want to know about the night King Barlow died. Addie has no recollection."

"Possibly that's for the best. We thought so at the time. Poor girl, she had been through hell."

"I might agree with you, except that she is still frightened. In some way, she still believes she was responsible for his death."

"Well, that is just not so. The inquest was quite clear on that point."

"She has terrible nightmares, Mr. Talbot, I'm sorry, Jim. She screams out in terror, pitiful, horrible screams. Sometimes I'm afraid that she'll never wake up, never be right again. I wouldn't ask if I didn't feel it was important. Perhaps if she knew what really happened, the dreams might stop. Maybe if I could reassure her. If it makes any difference, we are to be married soon. I love her very much. I'm just trying to help. You must understand that I would never do anything to hurt her."

"Has Mrs. Barlow told you much about her marriage?"

"About the abuse? Yes."

"Then, perhaps you're right. Perhaps you should know, but be forewarned, the truth is not pleasant."

"Before you begin, how did you come to learn about that night?"

"The housekeeper, Sally Mendoza. She came to me before the inquest. We made up the story together. We rehearsed it over and over. The doctor thought it best. Addie was so fragile and she agreed without comment.

"Mrs. Mendoza came to me, very distraught. She felt a great sense of loyalty to her employer. She had been with the Barlow family since her childhood, but the episode was so horrible, I don't think she could live with herself unless she told someone.

"She had apparently heard Mrs. Barlow's screams from the dining room, then silence. Her room was located just down the corridor from Addie's. When she peeked out her door a short time later, she spied the master carrying his wife into his room. She was clearly unconscious. Prior to this, Sally had heard a crash. She assumed he had knocked her out. As you probably know, it had happened a number of times before.

"Anyway, she waited a short time, and then crept out, afraid that Mrs. Barlow might need medical attention. Since this had happened before, her routine, if you want to call it that, was to ascertain that her employer was passed out for the night, then go to his wife's assistance. That night, King had appeared to be very drunk.

"When she reached the door, she peered in, expecting to see him lying in a stupor, stretched across the bed, the poor girl lying senseless beside him. What she found was Mrs. Barlow lying across the bed, still unconscious. Her clothes had been ripped to shreds and they lay scattered about the room, and the monster was on top of her, still awake."

Jim Talbot paused, his glasses misting over, "I'm sorry. Such unspeakable depravity, you see, King Barlow was raping his wife as she lay unconscious, bruised and hurt. She was, of course, completely defenseless. He had tied her hands and legs to the bedposts. Horrified, Sally ran back to her room and locked the door, not daring to venture forth until she heard screaming just before dawn.

"When she entered the bedroom, his bedroom, she found Mrs. Barlow, still tied to the bed posts, pinned underneath her husband's lifeless body. She was hysterical, in shock. Sally untied her and together they rolled his cold, already stiffening body off his shivering young wife. Sally bundled her mistress in blankets and took her to her own bed, then called the police.

"She gave her two of King's sleeping pills, a very strong dosage, I believe. When Addie woke, she remembered nothing. Not a blessed minute of it, thank God.

"We, Sally and I, assume that he died soon after Sally had peeped in the previous night, perhaps while still in the act of assaulting her. We assume that he… that the body lay on top of the poor senseless girl until she regained consciousness in the early morning. Poor creature had a severe concussion. It was a miracle that she woke up at all. The next few days were horrible for her. I don't doubt the nightmares continue. Her husband was a monster, Fielding, a cowardly, lecherous, brutal man, who deserved to die years sooner than he did. Apparently, he didn't treat the first Mrs. Barlow much better. Sally believed that he drove her insane, though the poor woman was supposed to have died of natural causes."

Ned wanted to ask a million questions. Why had this Mendoza woman continued to work for King Barlow after witnessing such barbarity? Why hadn't anyone else found out? Why hadn't he been stopped? How could such a monster have wooed and won the confidence and affection of his beautiful Addie? He wanted to ask, wanted to say something, but instead he sat, numb, his heart in his throat.

Finally, Talbot broke the silence. "Fielding, are you all right?"

Ned nodded weakly, aware of what he must look like to this kind stranger, who had taken time from his Saturday to meet with him.

"It was a long time ago. My advice would be to bury it. You've found each other and that is fortunate, indeed. Let the other go. No sense in dragging her through any of it again, the poor girl."

Ned rose and extended his hand. "Thank you, Jim. I appreciate your taking the time to see me."

"You look a little green around the gills. Would you like to stay for a bit? Have a cup of coffee? Perhaps the wife could fix you up a sandwich to take along with you?"

"I'm fine, thank you. I've disturbed you long enough. It's just that—"

"I know, a sickening, horrible business. Never heard the like of it again and hope I never do."

Talbot showed him out, a grimness clouding his boyish features. As they parted, he took hold of Ned's shoulder. "She's strong, your Addie, a fighter. He beat her many times over the years, I'm convinced of that. But you know, I don't believe he ever broke her spirit. Fact is, I believe that the wretch knew it, and beat her harder because of it."

Ned nodded and retreated to his car. He drove around the corner, out of sight, and then stopped and turned off the motor. Only then did he break down. Tears of rage washed over him, his shoulders heaving. After a long while, he recovered and began the drive back to Greenleaf. He couldn't wait to hold Addie again, to return to the only life he could imagine living. He was sure now. Surer than he'd ever been about anything, and he wanted to tell her.

CHAPTER 51

"You really have to go?"

"I really do, sweetheart. But thanks, Syd, for everything. It's been a great three weeks with you guys."

"And Christmas?"

"I hope so. I'll…we'll let you know."

"You sure about all this? I mean you've only known her a few months. Maybe you ought to wait a little, you know? Sometimes when people end relationships, like you and Mom, they go for the first person they see."

"It's not like that, honey. Believe me. Addie is, well, she's the one. I won't change my mind."

From across the breakfast table, his daughter regarded him in silence for several minutes. "You love her more than Mom, don't you?"

"Sydney, it's not that simple. Your mother and I, in the early years, when we had you and Ned, it was good. We were happy and in love."

"But not like this?"

"If you mean, was it the same? No. My relationship with Addie is different, very different, but don't forget, I'm twenty some years older, with a lot of living behind me. My perspectives and what I want out of life are different. There's no way to compare, so let's not. Okay?"

"Subject closed. When can I come and visit?"

"Anytime."

"How 'bout I tag along today?"

"Well, maybe give us a day or two."

"Just kidding, but I do want to meet her. Soon, Dad."

As he drove down the coast several hours later, Ned thought about his daughter, and about Janie and Ned. They'll love her, he told himself, why am I worrying? But, as he approached the village, worry and concern occupied his thoughts and he nearly missed the Tripp's Landing turn-off. What if she'd cried all night after the phone call? Had she spent the last few days heartbroken at the thought of leaving Winward? Where would he find her?

How selfish and stupid I've been, he chided himself, pulling up in front of the Rudder's boathouse. Now, on top of everything, Abe's gone home for the day and there's no one around to take me home. Marveling for an instant at the change in the village with its thick blanket of snow, he started up the street to the diner. He intended to call Rudder at home when a voice called from behind him, "Hey, Mr. Fielding!"

Turning, he spied Rufus, loping up from the dock, massive in his heavy winter jacket. "Hey, Rufus, how are you?"

"Fine, sir." The young man extended his hand and shook Ned's warmly. "Home for the holiday. Gotta go back in a couple of hours."

"How's it going?"

"Pretty good, 'cept for English. Addie, Mrs. Barlow helped me a lot. We've been workin' together the past two days. She helped me write a big term paper. Promised to help me some more when I need it."

"That's great, Rufus."

"She's nice. You were right about her. Even Pop's come around." Rufus smiled, an ironic, mischievous twinkle in his eye.

"So I heard," Ned said. "Listen, Rufus—I need to get out to the island, can you take me?"

"What happened to your canoe?"

"Belongs to SENCA. They took it back when the study was over."

"Then what are you doing back here?"

"Rufus, please. I need a ride. I'll rent a boat if you like, if that'd be easier."

"Hold yer horses, Mr. F. I'll take you. Let me call Pop to let him know I'll be a while."

"Thanks, Rufus."

Ned headed to the car to gather his things.

CHAPTER 52

They reached the island's dock in the dwindling daylight, long shadows playing in front of them as they unloaded Ned's few bags. The day had grown bitter cold with the approaching twilight and Ned shivered, his breath visible and his nose numb with cold.

"Shit, it's cold," he muttered, taking the last of the bags from Rufus.

"Yup, and I don't see no tent nor sleepin' bag here." Rufus said, as he pushed off. "Good luck, Mr. Fielding."

Ned waved, then turned away to shield his eyes as he scanned the cliffs. No sign of her. Grabbing the bags, he headed up the path towards the cottage. He expected to see her at any moment and was disappointed when she did not appear.

When he reached the clearing, he began to wonder if some accident might have befallen her. He had imagined Addie spending the day perched on the cliff waiting for him. Fool. Of course, she had better things to do.

As he neared the cottage, worry crept over him. Then Addie appeared and was running towards him, the blue of her sweater peeking out from under her heavy winter anorak. Dressed in blue jeans and hiking boots, her steps crunched over the thick layer of snow that covered the meadow. Dropping his bags, his parka slipping off along with his backpack, he ran to meet her. "Addie, my beautiful, darling Addie!"

He whirled her around, his arms encircling her slender form buried under layers of winter clothes.

She smiled, drawing back to survey him. "You'll get cold."

"Never."

He kissed her again and again, holding her close. Finally, they collected his bags and made their way towards the cottage, arm in arm. Aran raced around them, nipping playfully at their heels. The cook stove in the kitchen and a fire blazing on the hearth heated the house with unexpected warmth after the bitter cold of the outdoors. He peered through to the table, set with her best linens. Delicious aromas filled the house.

He dropped the bags just inside the door and their coats fell to the floor as they turned to face each other. Shy for an instant, they soon embraced, holding each other tightly.

"Oh, my darling, Addie, I've missed you so much." He buried his face in her neck.

"Me, too."

Ned carried her into the living room, one hand already inside of her sweater, running along the soft, smooth skin of her back, reaching around to caress her breasts. She shuddered and drew her arms around his neck as he slowly lowered her to the floor.

Undressing her, his kisses found every inch of her body, and she his as she simultaneously removed his clothes. He moaned, whispering, "Oh Addie, I want you so much."

"I love you," she whispered as she guided him into her deep, soft folds, hips reaching up to meet his every thrust, needing him every bit as much as he did her.

Afterwards, they lay warm and peaceful, entwined on the soft hearth rug. "This is the happiest moment of my life." He nuzzled her neck, then kissed her nose.

"Me, too," she smiled. "Did I tell you I love you, Mr. Fielding?"

He rose on one elbow and gazed down at her beautiful body stretched out beside him. "Mmm, but can you live with me?"

"Yes, anywhere."

Her eyes smiled back at him, vainly striving to hide the sadness he knew she felt.

"How 'bout here? Is there room for me here?"

For a moment, she didn't answer, just stared at him, incredulously, "I don't understand? Please Ned, don't tease me."

"I'm not teasing, my darling. I want to live right here, on Winward, if you'll have me. Presumptuous, huh? I don't ever want us to leave, except for vacations, of course. I can't promise I'll be the greatest farmer, or fisherman, but I'm willing to learn if you'll teach me."

"Oh, Ned!"

She threw her arms around him, sobs wracking her body.

"Hey, I thought it'd make you happy."

"I am happy," she sobbed, "I am."

"I know my sweet, beautiful darling, I know."

Epilogue

Addie and Ned were married on December 18th in the chapel at Saint Timo-thy's, Reverend Chase officiating. All three of Ned's children were present, Ned Jr., Janie and Sydney and a number of villagers as well. Afterwards, a simple reception was held in the parish house to celebrate the union. From there, the newlyweds departed for a brief honeymoon, at a small inn in New Hampshire. They returned in time to spend Christmas with Ned's children, all of them together at the Peterson estate. Penny and Martin Lawson, married two days before Christmas, had already departed for a honeymoon in Aruba.

Ned eventually told Addie what he learned from Jim Talbot, about the night of King's death. Terrible as it was, the truth seemed to calm her, to help put the horror behind her at last. As time went by, the nightmares lessened in severity, finally disappearing altogether to leave them in peace.

Addie had been right that day in April when she had furiously lashed at the water as she paddled her kayak. The island was never the same after Ned Fielding's arrival, but, unlike her sentiments on that day, she now seemed to welcome visitors and enjoyed the change in routine. She flourished in her life with Ned and enjoyed a happiness she had never thought possible.

Ned found great comfort and satisfaction in the natural rhythms and life of the farm. He enjoyed gardening and fishing and the winter chores of rebuilding and mending. Most of all, he loved the evenings spent with his wife, their love growing deeper as time went on. In the winter months, while Addie painted, Ned wrote and continued to publish and research.

Every summer, students and researchers came to the island to stay in the permanent shelter SENCA had erected in the meadow, not far from Ned's original campsite. A small, one-room cabin with an outhouse behind it, the building hunkered down into its surroundings and was barely visible beyond the reaches of the meadow. For the most part, SENCA people respected their privacy, and Addie and Ned, in turn, opened the eastern half of the island to their visitors, the tidal marshes providing a rich laboratory for study.

Janie and Ned visited that first summer with their daughter, Annabelle, and many more times over the years. Ned's children loved the island, and more importantly, they loved Addie. They had, in fact, taken to her from the start. He had never seriously doubted that they would, but their growing fondness for each other was a source of great comfort and joy to Ned. Like a sister more than a parent, she became a confidant to Sydney and a nurturing presence for all of them, especially the grandchildren. As the years went by, island vacations with Addie and Poppy, became the most special events in their year.

Ned often thought about his first days on the island, both the promise they'd held and the loneliness, never dreaming then that he would find such love and happiness on the isolated beauty of Winward Island. When they died, Addie first, then Ned three days later, they remained there still. Their descendants honored their final wish and their mingled ashes were scattered over the meadow where Ned had first told Addie that he loved her.

Please read on to preview chapters from Lee's mystery, *A Friend of Silence!*

Acknowledgements

I would like to thank Carol Entin, entomologist extraordinaire, for educating me about the habits of Nicrophorus Americanus, the American Carrion Beetle. A gifted teacher, Carol's enthusiasm for animals and the natural world, have enriched the lives of hundreds, maybe thousands, of fortunate students (including my two sons!) at Moses Brown School in Providence, Rhode Island. While any mistakes are entirely mine, Carol did provide valuable background about this fascinating species.

I continue to be grateful for the manuscript wizardry of the Formatting Fairies, and the unfailing good cheer and encouragement they bestow upon this fledgling author. Most importantly, I would like to thank my dear family and friends, who are always there, no matter where life's travels take me. I love them all beyond words. Finally, a huge thank you to my readers for picking up my books, for writing to tell me you love them, and for continuing to come back for more. It is heartwarming to know you are out there!

ABOUT THE AUTHOR

M. Lee Prescott is the author of numerous works of fiction for adults, young adults and children, among them **Prepped to Kill, Gadfly (Books One and Two in the Ricky Steele series), Jigsaw, A Friend of Silence,** and **Song of the Spirit.** Her newest contemporary romance series, **Morgan's Run**, debuts in the fall of 2014. Three of her nonfiction titles have been published by Heinemann and she has published numerous articles in the field of literacy education. Lee is a professor of education at a small New England liberal arts college where she teaches reading and writing pedagogy. Her current research focuses on mindfulness and connections to reading and writing. She regularly teaches abroad, most recently in Singapore.

Lee has lived in southern California (loved those Laguna nights!), Chapel Hill, North Carolina, and various spots in Massachusetts and Rhode Island. Currently, she resides in Massachusetts on a beautiful river, where she canoes, swims, and watches the incredible variety of migratory birds that pass by. She is the mother of two grown sons, Ransom and Winward, and spends lots of time with them, their beautiful wives, Alexandra and Stephanie, and her amazing grandchildren, Abigail, Ava and Benjamin. When not teaching or writing (both of which she loves), Lee's passions revolve around family, yoga (Kripalu is a second home), swimming, bouncing, and walking.

Lee loves to hear from readers. Visit her website at *mleeprescott.com* and Facebook page (mleeprescott). The Facebook page is a "work in progress," but I am working on it with help from friends who know what they are doing! Her e-mail is *mleeprescott@gmail.com*.

A Note from the Author

Thank you so much for taking the time to read **Widow's Island**. The seeds of Ned and Addie's story were planted many years ago when I read an article in the *Providence Journal* about the discovery of carrion beetles on a local island. What better place to set a romance between two wounded souls than a remote island, surrounded by an often-turbulent ocean? Although I live on a river, I return to the ocean often, as it is a place of profound peace and presence for me. The mythical creatures of Aran, Branwen and Gwydyon come from my love of the Welsh Mabinogion and the magical realism of the writers I adore.

If you liked **Widow's Island** and would be willing to write an Amazon review, I would very much appreciate it! In fact, I will be happy to send my first 25 reviewers a free e-copy of **another of my titles**! If you submit a review, just e-mail me at *mleeprescott@gmail.com* and I will see that you receive your free copy of whichever title you choose!

If you would like to sign up for future book releases and occasional notices about my books, please e-mail me at *mleeprescott@gmail.com* and I will add you to the list. I promise I will not share your address, nor will I flood you with e-mails. Do visit my website at *www.mleeprescott.com* to read more about my books and to hear what's next. **Lost in Spindle City**, the third in the Ricky Steele mystery series debuts this summer, and I am really excited about my upcoming romance series, **Morgan's Run**, set in the United States southwest, another special place I visit often. The first **Morgan's Run** title is scheduled for release in fall of 2014!

Finally, this book has been revised, proofed and edited many, many times, but I, and my intrepid assistants, are human, so if you spot a typo, please e-mail me at *mleeprescott@gmail.com* and I will fix it. If you'd like to know more about my other books, please scroll ahead to the next section that is followed by sample chapters of **A Friend of Silence**!

Warm wishes,
M. Lee Prescott

Contemporary romances and mysteries by M. Lee Prescott include:

Mysteries

The Ricky Steele series
Book 1: Prepped to Kill
Book 2: Gadfly
Book 3: Lost in Spindle City (coming summer of 2014!)

Also featuring Ricky Steele:
Jigsaw

Single titles

Romantic suspense
A Friend of Silence

Contemporary Romance
Swoon (coming soon!)
Glass Walls (coming soon!)
Morgan's Run

Young Adult Historical Romance
Song of the Spirit

SAMPLE : A FRIEND OF SILENCE
CHAPTER 1

Dry, cracked lips mouthed a silent scream as the old gardener cradled her lifeless body. Lizzie's ginger curls tangled in the gnarled fingers, silken threads catching on the rough, calloused hands. The dusky light was filtered through dense vines matting the roof of the long-abandoned greenhouse. A shaft of light struck his anguished face. The object of his grief lay in the shadows beneath him.

From his hiding place, Louie had watched uncomprehending, as she drank from the leather-bound flask, Macomber Dore's hiking flask. How it came to be in Lizzie's possession was never discovered. Soon after she set down the flask, Lizzie clutched at her throat, agony twisting her delicate features, hand sweeping clay pots from their shelves as she fell to the earthen floor.

Ferret-like, Louie had skittered from the shadows and rushed to her side. Now, he knelt holding her, shards of crockery cutting into his knees. He felt nothing, lost in a terrible grief from which his broken mind would never recover. He buried his face in the ginger locks, breathing in the scent of rose petals and jasmine. It seemed impossible that he would never again hear Lizzie's laugh…never hear her musical voice as she read aloud to him. Never feel her warm gaze like an embrace when she smiled at him.

Lizzie was dead, like the sparrows that crashed against the campus' picture windows, their little necks broken. How often had he lifted warm, downy bodies from the hard winter ground, held them as he now held his precious girl? His dearest girl was dead, like his dear mum years ago. On that steamy August night, Mum's unseeing eyes had stared up at him from where she lay, on faded grey linoleum, thrown there by his drunken father.

"She's gone. She's gone," he screamed, in the fading light…screamed and screamed until someone came running.

CHAPTER 2

Sunlight danced a frantic desperate reel as the shadow moved across the small, cluttered study. Salty breezes followed the intruder's footsteps into the room along with the fecund richness of fallen leaves, the earthy dampness creeping into every corner. Despite the cool wind, the thief wiped a trickle of sweat from brow, lifting the lid of the glass case with gloved hand.

The knife lay where it always lay, on decaying mauve velveteen long-since faded to gray. Like the silver pieces and other scrimshaw laying in the case beside it—letter openers, belt buckles and sperm whale teeth etched in a delicate hand—the knife looked neglected, forgotten. A gossamer veil of dust draped the antique cherry display case, obscuring the once-beloved collection. Mac would have never permitted such untidy housekeeping, but his widow didn't care, or more likely, didn't notice. The thief slipped the knife, sheath and all into the knapsack. As he lowered the lid, the creak of hinges echoed in the silence.

Brilliant choice for a murder weapon, the intruder mused. Not only did the knife have a firm, comfortable grip, but who in their right mind would believe Bess Dore capable of murder? There'd be trouble for her. She'd be questioned, of course, but eventually she'd be cleared with no harm done.

Crossing a sharp ray of afternoon sunlight, the thief squinted, before turning and slipping from the room through French doors that led onto the terrace. Thick shrubbery and grasping tendrils of Boston ivy shielded the terrace from view of the drive and the country road beyond. Acres of fields and woods stretched for miles behind the cottage, thus allowing the intruder to pass unseen.

A rusty bicycle borrowed from the school's bike rack waited, propped against a towering elm, its shady canopy casting a deep shadow over small side yard. Her backyard was dotted with hosta and canvas lawn chairs placed helter-skelter. The thief wove in and out around the obstacles, then regained the path leading out to the road. The lane was deserted, not a car to note the stranger's passing.

On the short ride back to campus, the knapsack swished from side to side, its knobby cargo grating and slapping against the cyclist's nylon windbreaker.

"Goodbye, Milt," the stranger whispered aloud, pedaling faster. "After tonight, the world will be a safer place at last."

CHAPTER 3

Carol Richards gazed out her office window spying Louie Predo, one of the school's gardeners as he rounded the classroom building perched atop the Graveley. Louie wasn't permitted to operate the big tractors, but the ancient Graveley and the gardener were of the same vintage and they knew each other well. The sight of the old man on the low, red lawn tractor put Carol in mind of a giant lobster, escaped from the nearby Atlantic. As she watched, Louie stopped at the corner of the building, leaping from the tractor. "What is that silly man up to?" she thought, stepping closer to the window.

Like most of the campus architecture, the two-story classroom building was a simple wood-frame design, finished with white clapboards. On each floor, eight-foot windows ran the length of building, their mullioned symmetry shutterless, in keeping with Quaker simplicity. A green skirting of shrubbery—boxwoods, yews and flowering azaleas, all well-established and carefully tended—ringed the building on all four sides.

The gardener began pawing and thrashing his way into the bush. Finally, he withdrew, a green book bag in his hand. Unzipping it, he peered inside. A long, curling ash had formed on the end of Carol's cigarette, but she didn't notice. Louie's back was turned away, his features unreadable, but fear registered in every inch of the thin, wiry frame as he flung the knapsack back into the shrubbery, jumped onto the tractor and drove away.

"Completely mad," she muttered, turning away. "Never been the same since that poor girl's death."

The year following Lizzie Mederois' suicide, enrollment had plummeted. She had been forced to work especially hard to make the budget stretch. There had been no putting anything by that year.

"Damn," she cried as the tube of ash fell down her sleeve, sprinkling the front of her blouse. New and expensive, the buttery-cream silk picked up the milky strands running through her tweed suit. She wasn't wearing the suit's jacket, since, as usual, the heat in the building was close to ninety. Carol liked things cool, but Milt, her assistant, was always turning up the heat. Insufferable toad, she thought, angrily brushing at her blouse. She simply could not abide the man.

Shrugging thoughts of the gardener and Milt Wickie from her mind, Carol began collecting her things to go home. A thick stack of papers lay waiting to be stuffed into her brown leather attaché, papers gathered in stealth. Their removal would help cover her tracks, moving her closer to the retirement she craved. She had only to deal with Milt. Once the little weasel handed over the last few documents, she'd be home free.

It had been so easy—the money and the rest, the school's antiques mysteriously disappearing a few at a time over the years, "into storage." Quakers were so trusting. She visualized the long deacon's table, now the centerpiece of her Cape Cod dining room. It had been taken out for repair during the Coop's renovation years ago and had simply vanished. Once all the modern furnishings arrived, no one seemed to remember or care about the priceless table. Then, there was the rare Goddard highboy, sent out for repairs and, alas, destroyed in a fire at the refinisher's; it looked gorgeous in the foyer of her Boston brownstone.

She loved the brownstone, purchased with her cut of the school's last capital campaign. Living in the city would be heaven after Hicksville. It was an expensive address, but she'd earned every penny, deserved every cent. Of course, the art studio expansion had been scaled down a little to keep up with the brownstone's mortgage, but since she kept the books, no one was the wiser. Certainly not the little brats who trashed the place. In no time at all, the studio's lovely white walls and soft gray carpets were blotched and stained under their careless tenancy. Carapaldi Construction had rewarded her with a handsome dividend after they received that contract.

Soon, the good life would be hers. No more endless meetings, no more wrangling with the Board, no more being roused in the middle of the night to respond to a foolish prank in the dorm. Now that life beyond Old Harbor Friends was in her grasp, she would not let boorish Milt spoil things. He'd had his chance years ago and he'd blown it, throwing her over for a new conquest. Why, the man had a new tart practically every week. Carol had long since stopped counting. Insatiable, that's what he was. He'd even made a play for goody-goody, Bess Dore, still mourning her dreary clod of a husband, after what, ten years?

Milt had had his chance, but now it was too late. Let him threaten, let him try to stop her and he'd discover just who he was dealing with. Snapping the briefcase shut, she swished out of the office, leaving every light on and the door wide open. "Let the night watchman close up," she muttered. "Let him earn the exorbitant wage we pay him."

Once outside, distant sounds of a tractor reminded her of the gardener and she took a detour on her way across campus, pausing to peer into the boxwood. Search as she might, she could find no trace of the green knapsack. Finally, hands scratched and panty hose snagged, she withdrew, cursing herself for stopping. Brushing off, she headed home to her lonely, gray-walled apartment on the third floor of George Foxe Hall. Sixty-two adolescent girls lived on the floors below her, but she had little to do with them. Her stint of dorm duty had mercifully ended years ago.

As she climbed the stairs, anticipating the gloom waiting in her drafty rooms, she smelled fresh popcorn and cookies baking. The muffled cacophony of voices as girls returned from sports practice faded along with the delicious scents as she reached the third floor landing. Shivering, she slipped her key into the lock. Turning her back on the warmth below, Carol Richards stepped into a bleak world, her home for the past twenty years.

www.ingramcontent.com/pod-product-compliance
Lightning Source LLC
Chambersburg PA
CBHW061027120726
47910CB00006B/2139